THE CAPTAIN'S CHRISTMAS PROMISE

THE CAPTAIN'S CHRISTMAS PROMISE

Griffin Force

JULIE COULTER BELLON

Copyright © 2020 by Julie Coulter Bellon.

Published by Stone Hall Books

Cover Design by Steven Novak Illustrations

ISBN 10: 1-7363129-0-1

ISBN 13: 978-1736312902

Printed in the United States of America

First Printing December 2020

10 9 8 7 6 5 4 3 2 1

ACKNOWLEDGMENTS

This book came to me out of the blue, while we were on a roadtrip. It wouldn't leave me alone for the entire ride, so I knew I had to write it!

I need to thank Jon, Jeni, Jodi, and Annette who are always up for reading the manuscript in various stages and making it better than it was. I'm so grateful to have my team behind me! Thank you for all you do for me.

I also need to thank my SWAT team for their tireless efforts. I truly am blessed to have so many amazing people that support me.

This has been a crazy year and my family has been incredibly patient. I'm so grateful for their love and encouragement. There's no one else I'd rather be quarantined with!

CHAPTER ONE

Colt's head was starting to throb. He'd been staring at the computer screen for hours, and the words were starting to blur. Nazer al-Raimi, one of the most wanted terrorists in the world, had briefly surfaced in Paris. The entire Griffin Force team was tracking down leads, reaching out to contacts and verifying intel to get a lock on his location. Colt had been combing through bank accounts and transactions that were linked to Nazer, but the task was slow and time-consuming. Everything that would make it hard for a sleep-deprived operative to concentrate. But it would all be worth it if they could pinpoint a location and grab Nazer.

After what had happened in Afghanistan, there wasn't anything Colt wanted more than to have Nazer al-Raimi in custody. He had a score to settle.

"Hey." Brenna walked through his open office door

and bent to give him a quick kiss. "You look like you could use a break."

Having her so close kicked his heart rate up a notch, and suddenly he didn't feel quite so tired. "Yeah? That bad?" He pushed back from the table and stood.

She ran her hands over his shoulders. "You fishing for compliments?" Her fingers slipped down his biceps, and he shifted closer to her.

"No, but I'll take one if you're dishing them out." He took her hand in his and looked into her eyes as he tugged her to him. Reaching up to run his thumb over her cheek, he shifted his hand to cup her head and inch her even closer. Her eyes darkened and she leaned in until there wasn't any space between them. Lightly pressing his mouth to hers, he teased her lips, the world narrowing down to just the two of them. She wrapped her arms around his neck and deepened the kiss, his heart rate racing as he matched her intensity. When they broke apart, her breaths were coming fast.

"I need to sit down," she said touching her forehead to his. "My knees are feeling a bit weak all of a sudden."

"Best compliment I've heard all day." He grinned as she pulled the chair out next to him and got comfortable.

Maneuvering the chair close to the table, she glanced over at the laptop he'd been working on. "Any luck tracing the bank statements to Nazer?"

"No." He sat back down and rolled his neck. "If he's

using any of these accounts in France, I can't find the connection."

"Maybe we should get some coffee, and then I'll help you look." She reached out and took his hand. "Although I do think you need to sleep. You've barely closed your eyes the last two days."

"I'm fine." He squeezed her fingers. "I don't want to miss our chance to get Nazer and take him down. Did you have any luck with your contacts?"

She took a breath and her gaze dropped to the table, like she was reluctant to tell him. "A few leads, actually. We're checking them out."

"What have we got? Maybe I can help." His energy level seemed to ratchet up at her words. Maybe fresh intel was exactly the break they needed.

"We won't know anything for a couple of hours. Why don't you catch a nap? I'll wake you if anything happens." She lifted her eyes to his, and he could see her concern. It warmed him. He couldn't remember the last time he'd had someone worry over him in the field. Everyone just did their jobs and was grateful to come back alive after the mission.

He lifted her hand to his lips and kissed her knuckles. "You don't have to worry. I'm okay."

Brenna reached up with her other hand and let her fingers trail down the still-visible bruise on his jaw from their last op. "Your injuries aren't going to heal if you don't give them a chance."

"I'm okay. I promise." Colt wanted to take her in his arms again and kiss all that worry away.

Brenna looked like she was about to say more, but Julian appeared in the doorway, heaving out a sigh. "None of our leads have panned out. All we've been able to do is confirm he was in the 20th district last night, but he isn't there anymore. What if Nazer figured out we're tracking him and went to ground?" Julian rubbed his neck. "If that's what's happened, we're going to have to start from scratch. Augie thinks he would try to get to Pakistan, since he has a network there, but we're going to have to start reaching out to our contacts for any confirmation."

Colt's stomach sank, and he closed his eyes. He'd needed a win tonight. Every exhausting minute he'd been fighting through came to the fore. All their work and effort, but Nazer had gotten away. Again. "How could he know we were tracking him? Do you think someone tipped him off?"

"The man does have spies everywhere." Brenna turned to Julian. "What do you think?"

Julian sank down into the chair next to Colt. "Sometimes I feel like we're chasing our tails."

Brenna shook her head. "We aren't. We've made progress. We've infiltrated his organization before, foiled his terrorist activities. He's on the run, and that's a good thing. We just have to be patient about bringing him in."

Colt was at the end of his patience, though. He

clenched his fists. They should have had Nazer several times over, but he always managed to slip away. "You're right. We've just got to keep on him. Do whatever we have to do to find him."

Julian shifted forward in his chair. "Actually, you haven't slept or eaten anything beyond a donut for nearly forty-eight hours. You won't be any good to us if you collapse from exhaustion. You need a break to take care of yourself."

Colt's eyes met Brenna's, silently asking if she'd voiced her concerns to Julian, but she gave him a slight shake of her head. She hadn't. "I'm fine," he said, turning to face Julian. "Really."

"I'm giving you some time off," Julian said, his tone firm. "How long has it been since you were home for Christmas?"

"A few years. But my family understands." Though, ever since his brush with death in Nazer's compound, Colt had been thinking about his family more. It had been a while since they'd been in the same time zone. They would be ecstatic to have him home for the holidays. "I don't want any special treatment, Julian. If everyone else is staying, and the team needs me here, I'm happy to stick around."

Julian rubbed his jaw as he watched Colt, his eyes shadowed with concern and respect, but also warmth for his colleague and friend. "No special treatment, just an order to go home, rest up. We'll call you if anything changes with Nazer." Julian stood and put his hands in his pants pockets. "No sense in all of us missing Christmas with family around. Oh, and take Brenna with you. She'll just worry if she's stuck here without you."

Brenna smiled at their team leader. "You've really thought this through."

Julian chuckled, folding his arms and leaning against the doorjamb. "That's why I'm in charge, I guess."

"When can we leave?" Brenna pulled the laptop closer and started shutting it down. Colt thought about protesting, but from the determined look on her face, he wouldn't get very far.

Julian raised his eyebrows at her obvious eagerness. "Glad someone has the sense not to look a gift horse in the mouth. I can have the plane ready in a couple of hours."

"But you'll call me if there's any change in the Nazer situation?" Colt wanted to be sure he wasn't left out. There was no way he'd miss being there when they captured Nazer.

"You'll be kept in the loop. Now get out of here and say hi to your parents for me." Julian nodded and left.

"Your mom is going to be so excited." Brenna turned in her chair to face Colt, her eyes fairly dancing with happiness. Colt hadn't seen that look for a long time. The light in her face warmed his heart.

"Yeah, she will be. My dad and Emily, too." Colt couldn't remember when he'd last had a Christmas tree or opened presents on Christmas morning with his family. He hadn't realized how much he missed it. Maybe taking a step back from tracking Nazer and going home was exactly what he needed after all. He could probably use a new perspective. "Should I surprise her?"

Brenna took his hand in hers. "That's a great idea. You'd be the best Christmas present she'll get this year."

Colt could already imagine showing up at his parents' door. His mom would probably be baking something or decorating for Christmas. She loved decorating and went all out with a real, pine-smelling tree, popcorn strings around it, bulbs his grandparents had decorated their tree with, and an angel on the top that always went on last. His dad would be busy stringing the lights and trying to fix the one string that was always out. Colt rubbed his chin. His sister Emily had just turned fifteen. The last Christmas he'd spent with her, she'd been excited about getting a doll. Her ten-year-old squeals when she opened the very one she'd wished for still echoed in his memory. Now she'd probably want a new phone or a laptop or something. How had it been that long?

He pushed away from the table and leaned forward in his chair, moving closer to Brenna.

"What about your dad? Do you want to surprise him, too?"

Brenna's family only lived a couple of hours away from his. Colt remembered Brenna's mom as a go-getter before she passed away from cancer, and her dad as a gruff former soldier that lived for chess and fishing. They'd both been fiercely proud of their daughter, which had been evident from the first moment he'd met them years ago. Her dad had asked point blank what Colt's intentions were regarding Brenna. Maybe now Colt could give him a different answer. Something more than, "we're just dating."

But the twinkle in Brenna's eyes clouded over at the mention of her father. "He . . . Actually, he moved recently." She didn't meet his gaze, and her shoulders hunched slightly. Something was wrong.

"Where did he move to?" Colt scooted his chair closer to hers until their knees were touching.

"Hamilton." She was still avoiding his gaze, looking at the table instead.

He reached out and touched her back, moving his hand in soothing circles. "I can't imagine he'd like the city too much. He loved that little ranch."

"Yeah, he did." She swallowed and her voice sounded shaky. When she finally lifted her face, her eyes were full of tears.

Brenna rarely cried. Alarm tingled over him. "What's wrong?" She'd already lost her mother. Having something happen to her dad would crush her.

"He moved to assisted living a few months ago." She wiped away a tear that had escaped down her cheek. "It's actually residential care for Alzheimer patients."

A pit formed in Colt's stomach. He couldn't imagine

watching one of his parents go through that. His fingers tightened on hers. "Bren, why didn't you tell me?"

"There wasn't really time while we were trying to get you out of Afghanistan alive and,"---her voice got softer---"I'm having a hard time thinking of him there instead of at home."

As an intelligence officer, Brenna had been trained to compartmentalize her feelings, but something this big would be incredibly hard to contain. Colt couldn't even imagine the effort it would take to try to deal with all the emotions this would bring up and still get her assignment done while working in the field.

"I'm sorry. I wish I could have been there for you." Colt's tone matched hers, as if talking about this in hushed tones somehow made it easier to say.

"You're here now." She sniffed and he stood, taking her in his arms and holding her close.

"We can still go see him when we go home. A visit would be good for both of you." He felt a tremor go through her, and held her tighter.

"Sometimes I still call the old home number, and then I remember he's not there. He was forgetful, which happens at his age, but then he started forgetting the names of his friends he's had for decades, and he . . . he just wasn't himself." Brenna turned her head and pressed her face into his neck. "Before I went under-cover, I made arrangements for him. He just couldn't take care of himself anymore. But I found a great place, and he seems to like it. I . . . I have a hard time talking to him now. Sometimes he remembers who I am, and sometimes he doesn't."

Her voice was barely more than a whisper, and Colt had to lean close to hear. "So you haven't been home to see him? Since he moved?"

"No, we've just talked on the phone." She pressed her lips together and exhaled slowly through her nose. "And he begs me to take him home every time we talk. It breaks my heart."

Colt's heart broke hearing the pain in her voice. "Let's go see him for Christmas. Together." He squeezed her hand. "Maybe going home is just what we all need right now."

Maybe seeing him and reassuring herself that he was well taken care of would help both of them adjust. And Colt wanted to be there and help her through this. Whatever she needed. "Let's go home."

Brenna nodded and claimed a quick kiss before giving him a watery smile. "I'll go pack. Maybe you can sleep on the plane."

"If that's what makes you happy, I will sleep the entire way to Canada." He put his arm around her and they walked out of the office.

"As long as you don't keep me awake with your snoring." She gave him a sly smile. "A girl needs her beauty rest."

He squeezed her shoulder. "If you're only sleeping

for beauty benefits, you don't ever need to sleep again. You're beautiful just the way you are."

She grinned, just as he'd hoped and they headed down the hall. For the first time in years, Colt was looking forward to Christmas.

It was going to be unforgettable. He could feel it.

CHAPTER TWO

Brenna descended the stairs of Julian's private jet and walked onto the tarmac. She drew in a lungful of crisp Canadian air. It had been a long time since she'd been home during the winter. After her stints in the Middle East, the chill in the air was welcome.

She glanced over her shoulder at Colt---his head turned up to the blue sky while he breathed deeply. She smiled at the sight of it. "Feels good to be home, doesn't it?"

He moved next to her and put his arm around her shoulders. "It feels good to be here with you."

Tucking herself into his side, they walked toward the hangar. The snowplows must have been out early today because all the snow was scooped into mounds on the edges of the airfield. This was a smaller, private airfield, with just six runways. Julian must have pulled some strings to have them dropped here. The location was an hour closer to Colt's parents, and it would be a lot easier to get there without having to deal with security, customs, and the hundreds of people at the Toronto airport.

Two cars were parked near the hangar, a smaller four-door sedan and a black SUV. Brenna looked between the vehicles, hoping that the four-door was for them. The team often traveled in SUVs when they were on operations. For this trip, she wanted to feel like a civilian, and a smaller car would help with that.

As she drew closer, she noticed two men in suits loading luggage into the back of the SUV. They both had close-cropped hair and muscular physiques, but it was their stance and the way they kept an eye on the perimeter while they finished their task that gave them away as military. There was also an obvious bulge under one of the men's jackets, which meant he was carrying a gun. But who were they? And what were they doing here?

Colt didn't seem to notice the men at the SUV. He was focused on the man unloading their suitcases from Julian's plane. "I'm going to make sure our luggage gets to the car," Colt said, kissing her head before he moved away.

Brenna stopped and turned, shielding her eyes. She ran a quick perimeter check herself, but nothing seemed amiss. Two private planes were parked at the end of separate runways. Two cars waited near the hangar. That was it. Perhaps the men were security for a celebrity? Or a government official? As that thought crossed her mind, a man exited the second plane, put on a pair of aviator sunglasses, and started to walk toward her. He was lean, tanned, and his dark hair was windblown and rumpled, with a bit of stubble on his jaw. His royal-blue Henley shirt looked brand new as did his darker blue coat. This had to be the guy with the security detail.

She turned away and kept walking toward the hangar, but the man's long strides quickly caught up with her. "A beautiful day *and* a beautiful lady. I'm a lucky man," he said, running a hand through his hair and cocking his head to the side.

Brenna nodded politely. "It *is* a beautiful day," she agreed. His sunglasses hid his eyes, but there was no doubt his entire focus was on her.

"This is my first visit to Canada. And so far, it's been spectacular." He moved ahead of her and blocked her way. "My name is Jassim." He smiled and leaned closer. She could smell alcohol on his breath and groaned inwardly. She did not need this today. What was taking Colt so long? "And what is your name, beautiful lady?" he added.

Brenna turned all her attention to Jassim. She didn't feel threatened, necessarily, but she wanted to be careful. "I'm Brenna. But you'll have to excuse me." She moved around him and started walking again. He easily kept pace with her.

She glanced over at him. How drunk was he? He was walking a straight line for the most part, but the man certainly wasn't getting any of her hints.

"I know this is quite forward, but would you happen to be available to show me around this beautiful country? You're the first Canadian I've met, and I'd like to know you better." He gave her a wide smile. "Don't say no."

For someone who'd had a little too much to drink, he still had a bit of charm about him, like a little lost boy. But why did he need a security detail? If she wasn't mistaken, his name and accent were Middle Eastern. And his clothing and shoes told her he had money. She searched her memory and couldn't recall any diplomats or celebrities named Jassim. Who was he really?

"Didn't your mother teach you not to talk to strangers?" she asked, keeping her voice light.

"Yes, but she didn't say anything about *beautiful* strangers." He stopped her again, reaching out to touch her forearm. "We would have fun, I can promise you that."

Brenna tried to step back, but he suddenly gripped her hard. She looked down at his hand, then back up at him. "Jassim, let go of me."

"Come now, beautiful Brenna. Let's get to know each other better." His words slurred a bit and Brenna had had enough. She grabbed his arm and twisted it behind his back, holding his wrist at an angle that could snap it.

"Hey! Let go of me!" he protested. "What are you doing?"

The guards were running toward them now, guns drawn. "Release him!" the closest one shouted.

Brenna ignored the command. Keeping her hold on Jassim, she patiently waited until the guards surrounded them. It didn't take long. They pulled Jassim from her grasp, but kept their guns pointed at her chest.

Jassim rolled his shoulder and flexed his hand. "I'm okay," he said a little too loudly to his guards. "It's fine."

"My name is Brenna Wilson," she told the guards, holding up both of her hands in a show of surrender. "I'm unarmed."

Colt was coming toward them at a dead run. "Brenna!"

The shorter guard turned his gun on Colt. "Stop!" the guard demanded. "Stop right there!"

Colt slowed down, but kept moving toward her, his hands up. "I'm Commander Colt Mitchell. What's going on here?" He was totally focused on the men with the guns, assessing the situation and threat. Brenna moved toward him as well. They worked best as a team, so the closer they were, the better she felt.

The guards looked at each other, unspoken communication flowing between them before they lowered their weapons and spoke rapidly to each other in Arabic. A decision was made, and the taller one turned to them.

"We're sorry for any misunderstanding," he said. He'd spoken a more classical dialect of Arabic. If Brenna had to guess, he was from the Arabian Peninsula, probably Qatar or Kuwait. She remained silent, and he gave her one last assessing look before he holstered his gun. Taking Jassim's arm, he towed him closer to the SUV. "We must go now," he said with a nod. Brenna couldn't tell if he was talking to her or Jassim. Either way, it was easy to see the guards were anxious to have their charge in the car.

Jassim shook off the guard's hand and glared at him angrily, but the guard didn't even flinch, just shepherded their group toward the SUV. Colt and Brenna watched them load up and drive away.

"What was that about?" Colt asked as he touched her shoulder. "You okay?"

"Yeah." She turned toward him. "He's had a little too much to drink is all." She let out a breath, willing her heart rate to slow to a normal rhythm.

Colt pulled her to his chest and ran his hand over her back, as if to reassure himself she was really okay. "I about lost a year off my life seeing them pull guns on you. I thought we left all that behind in Afghanistan." He rested his chin lightly on the top of her head. "You were only on Canadian soil for fifteen minutes."

"Are you saying I attract trouble?" Brenna closed her eyes and slowly inhaled, enjoying being in his arms. "Need I remind you who got *you* out of trouble while we were on operations?" She leaned back slightly to look in his face and raised her eyebrows.

"Oh, I freely admit it was you." He bent to give her a quick kiss on the lips. "But I'll happily volunteer to keep you out of any and all trouble for the rest of the trip. The only catch is that you'll have to stay within arms-length of me at all times."

She laughed, sliding her fingers down his shoulder before she took his hand. "Okay, deal, but we better get on the road. I don't want to be knocking on your mother's door at midnight."

They walked to the car, and he opened the passenger door for her, then circled to the driver's side. It didn't take long before they'd left the airport behind, and were on the road to Rockwood where his family lived.

"Are you sure your parents will be okay that I'm tagging along?" Now that they were really here, Brenna's doubts were creeping back in. Maybe surprising his family hadn't been the best idea after all.

Colt smiled. "Of course. For a long time after we broke up, my mom would ask if I'd seen you. Now I can say yes."

That's what she was afraid of. Brenna turned to look out the window. "Was she upset about how things ended between us before?"

Colt reached over and took her hand. "You don't have to worry. She just wants me to be happy. And I am." He lifted her palm to his lips and kissed it.

Brenna wanted to believe that. She needed Colt's mother to like her.

"I can hear you worrying from here," Colt said, squeezing her fingers. "She's going to love you."

He let her hand go briefly while he turned the radio on. Christmas music filled the car, the familiar tune helping Brenna to relax. This was going to be fine. They were together. It was Christmas.

What could go wrong?

CHAPTER THREE

The sun was beginning its descent into the horizon, giving the snow on either side of the freeway an extra sparkle. The lull of driving slowly unwound the tension Colt had felt since seeing guns pointed at Brenna at the airport. The cars around them were thinning out, but there were still a few on the road. Colt glanced in the rearview mirror and saw the black sedan still behind them. The other driver was maintaining about the same distance between them and never attempted to pass. If he'd still been with the team hunting Nazer, Colt would have thought he was being followed. But they were in Canada now. They were off the clock, the risks were low, and he needed to relax.

Brenna turned the radio station from Christmas music to the news. "I haven't seen a weather report, have you? I wonder what we're in for."

As if the announcer had heard her question, he warned people of a winter storm rolling in that night with frigid temperatures. Once he finished, he ran down the day's top headlines. The Emir of the state of Kuwait, Sheik Karam al-Marisi, was in the country to discuss his humanitarian efforts for the Syrian refugees with the Prime Minister.

That means heightened security in Ottawa, Colt mused. He glanced over at Brenna, who was reaching to turn the radio station again.

"I'm not going to think about security, intelligence, or anything else except spending Christmas with our families," she muttered.

"It's like we're the moths, and any shred of international headlines is the light that we can't resist. We have to know what's going on behind the scenes to keep everyone safe." Colt came up behind a slower car and waited until they moved onto the shoulder slightly before he passed them. The black sedan behind them kept pace. Colt tensed, then forced himself to relax again. They were not being followed. Everything was fine.

Brenna sighed and hunched in her seat, as if the weight of the world was resting on her. "After the Legislature bombings, everyone will still be on high alert. And to have a visiting sheik, well, that puts an extra edge on every piece of chatter they'll be picking up. I imagine the Americans are also going to be watching closely, too, because if anything happened to al-Marisi while he's here . . ." She shook her head. "Maybe we should see if Julian has an update about Nazer."

"Do you think Nazer would have an interest in al-Marisi?" Colt turned the radio off and glanced at her. "You're not just chasing ghosts, are you? Seeing Nazer around every corner?"

"Nazer is all about pleasing his followers. If he can hit a member of a Kuwaiti royal family while abroad, especially one whose been trying to broker a peace deal in Syria, he'll do it. Plenty of terror groups in Syria would back that play." Brenna folded her arms and turned away to look out the window. "If anything happened to al-Marisi while he was on Canadian soil . . . that would be a huge blow, especially when we're still recovering from the Parliament bombings."

"Hey." He held his hand out and she interlaced her fingers with his. Running a thumb over her knuckles, he straightened and shifted closer. "We have to trust in our military and intelligence. They'll be on top of this."

"I know." She squeezed his fingers. "Sometimes I like to think that if I'm there, I'll see things no one else does and be able to stop it."

"I get that. But we can't be everywhere." He looked in his rearview mirror. The black car was still behind them.

"Looking at our tail?" Brenna asked, quirking an eyebrow at him. "What do you think that's about?"

Colt blew out a breath and looked in the rearview

mirror again. "I've been trying to convince myself that it's not a tail."

"Well, both of us are thinking the same thing, so we probably better take a closer look." She pointed to the gas station coming up on the next exit. "Pull off and we'll separate. You confront them, and I'll come up behind."

Colt frowned. They had no idea what they'd be facing with whoever this was. "How about you confront them and *I'll* come up behind?"

She shook her head and gave him a half smile. "I think you need a chance to brush off the rust and do a takedown."

He raised his eyebrows at her teasing. "Rust? Wow. Did you really just say that?"

She pressed her lips together to suppress a smile and shrugged her shoulders. "If the shoe fits."

He couldn't resist a laugh. "Okay, I'll accept your challenge and prove there's not a bit of rust on me." He accelerated a little bit as they exited the freeway. If they were going to do a split takedown, they'd need every second. "I wish I had my gun."

Her smile vanished. "This isn't exactly the Christmas vacation we envisioned. Who knew we would need our guns with us?" As soon as Colt stopped the car, Brenna unbuckled her seat belt. They didn't have much time. "Ready?"

"Be careful," he said as he opened his door. There

were so many variables, and they were going into this blind.

She nodded and he watched her run around the side of the building. Colt went into the little store that connected to the gas station, acknowledging the attendant. He headed down the hallway where the restrooms were. He made sure the back door to the store was open in case he needed a second exit strategy or Brenna needed a way in. Once that was done, he moved into the employee break room, which had a clear line of sight on the front door.

He didn't have to wait long. A man came in, obviously searching the place. He had a black toque pulled halfway down his forehead, and a matching black coat with the collar up. He circled the store, then headed to the back toward Colt.

Retreating into the shadows, Colt let the guy get close to the break room before he popped the door open. The guy started with surprise. Before he could turn around, Colt pinned him face first against the wall. Getting him into a chokehold took a lot more effort than Colt was anticipating. The guy was employing counter-maneuvers and was a lot stronger than he looked.

"My name is Sam," the guy choked out. "I work with your old commander, Lieutenant-Colonel Hayes." He twisted around, trying to get some leverage on Colt and slip out of the hold he had on him. "I need to talk to you."

He worked with Hayes? Colt eased up. He hadn't been expecting that. Brenna appeared in the hallway and took in the scene. "He was alone," she reported.

Colt allowed the man to stand straight. Turning him around slowly, but staying on alert, he looked him in the face. "How do you know Colonel Hayes?"

"He's my commanding officer, too," Sam said. "I'm in his communication unit. You can call and verify with him if you need to."

Colt searched the other man's eyes, trying to get a read on him. His close-quarters fighting experience was consistent with being a JTF2 operator. "You can verify it right now. What's the one name you'd never want to call Hayes to his face?"

Rolling his shoulders, Sam grinned. "His legal first name: Sheldon."

Colt stuck out his hand and the men shook on it. "Only a team guy or his lawyer would know that. So tell me, what are you doing here? And why are you following us?"

Sam looked down the hall and saw the attendant watching them. After giving him a thumbs up to let him know there was no trouble, Sam turned back to Colt and lowered his voice. "We've got a problem that I need to talk to you about. It involves national security. Can we go somewhere and talk? Please?"

Colt gave Brenna a questioning look, and she responded with a slight nod. "Yeah. Let's go."

Leading the way back outside, Sam motioned for

them to get in the backseat of his car two parking spots over from their four-door sedan. "It won't take long."

Colt opened the door, and Brenna slid in. Once they were settled, Sam turned to face them from the driver's seat. "I couldn't believe it when I saw you two at the airport. I followed you to validate that you were who I thought you were. I mean, what are the chances that we would be getting intelligence on the contract killing of Jassim al-Marisi, with a possible Nazer al-Raimi connection, and you all show up at the same airport? Something had to be up. But now I think it was just meant to be." He blew out a breath.

"Whoa, let's back up. Jassim is the sheik's son? And there's a hit out on him?" Brenna leaned forward and gripped the edge of the seat in front of her, focusing in on Sam. "What are you doing about it?"

Sam took off his toque and ran his hand through his hair. He clenched his jaw as he looked between her and Colt, obviously trying to choose his words carefully before he spoke. "This is highly classified information, but when I called in, Hayes gave you temporary clearance. We need your help." Sam turned as much as he could to face Colt. "The second it got out that Jassim was joining his father at the summit with the Prime Minister, chatter ramped up on all the terrorist networks that there would be an attempt on his life. But we couldn't verify anything specific."

Colt nodded. That was pretty standard for any visiting dignitaries with high profiles. All the intelligence agencies would have been working overtime on that front. "But now you've got a credible threat against him?"

"Yes." Sam's whole body seemed to tense. "And it's going to happen soon. In the next twenty-four hours."

Brenna sat back in her seat and folded her arms. "When we saw him at the airport, he only had two bodyguards. I'm surprised that Jassim isn't traveling with a bigger security team. Sheiks are usually pretty strict about personal protection when they travel, especially if the diplomatic visit is high profile."

Sam shifted in his seat and faced front, staring out the windshield. "Jassim is trying to separate himself from his father and prove his independence. He didn't feel it was necessary for anything other than his usual personal security detail. Hayes sent me to escort him from the airport, but he'd landed early. You two were still there, and going in the same direction he had, so I took a chance that maybe we could work together and track him down."

"I thought the sheik was just here to discuss humanitarian aid to Syria from Canada and Kuwait," Colt put in. His hand tapped his thigh, trying to see the situation from all angles. Why would anyone want to threaten al-Marisi?

"He *is* here for aid talks, but the sheik is also trying to bring the Syrian war to an end with a peaceful resolution. He's reached out to the Syrian government, the rebels, the jihadis, anyone who is involved and will talk to him, but that's made him a few enemies along the way." Sam looked at his watch and gave a sharp exhale. "I need to check in with Hayes and give him your answer."

Colt looked at Brenna. She was quiet, probably thinking of all the intel possibilities and contacts she could pull for this if they did agree to help. "Do you have any more information about the threat itself?" he asked.

"The specific threat is that the sheik will have his son's blood on his hands unless he stops his negotiations for peace in Syria." Sam did a quick glance outside the car, before he turned back to them. He was getting antsy. "We think the hitman is a Russian mercenary, former Special Forces, and we're using all our resources to find any hint as to his contacts here and how he was smuggled into the country. Did you have any direct contact with Jassim at the airport?"

Brenna kept her eyes on Sam. "Briefly. But his two bodyguards hustled him into a black SUV and they drove off." She didn't mention their little altercation, and Colt didn't feel the need to elaborate. "The guards seemed competent and were armed. Maybe they'll get in contact with you or Hayes when they get where they're going."

"I'll feel better if I *know* where they're going. I don't have to tell you what a diplomatic nightmare it would be if something happened to him while his father is here on a humanitarian mission." Sam rubbed a hand over his neck with a frown, as if imagining that scenario. "His father is insisting we bring him in immediately, which is what we all want."

"What do you need from us?" Colt knew what Sam was probably going to say, but wanted to hear it anyway. It was always good to have mission specifics before you jumped in on an op.

"Help me track Jassim down and bring him to Ottawa." Sam twisted in his seat so he could look at both of them. "I know you're with Griffin Force now, but you're two of the very best we've ever trained in military operating and intelligence. It was like Christmas came early when I saw you guys at the airport."

Colt rubbed his chin, thinking about his family, Brenna's dad, and the reason they'd actually come to Canada. "You know, we'd love to help, but Hayes has dozens of other trained officers who can step in. Jassim has two bodyguards with him and can't have gone far. We're here to take a bit of time off and see our families before we're back overseas with our own team."

"I understand that, but I need you. The country needs you." Sam's gaze pinned Colt. "This is time-sensitive. It would take too long to call anyone else down here, and the leads we have would be cold if we waited. We think he's headed to a luxury cabin on Silver Mountain to meet some friends and enjoy the snow. Intel suggested that the cabin is only accessible with a snowmobile, which is a security nightmare. An isolated cabin is the perfect place to execute a hit and make a clean getaway." He grimaced. "You know I wouldn't ask if I had any other options"

Brenna touched Colt's arm and gave him an apologetic look. "Colt, I know I've been the one saying we need a break and a step back, but what if Nazer is involved in this? If we find Jassim quick, we can still make it to your family's house late tonight for Christmas Eve or early tomorrow for Christmas day." She tilted her head and gave him a small smile.

"All right, I'm in if you're sure about this. I seem to remember someone talking about sleeping in, getting perspective and lots of rest . . . " He let his voice trail off.

She rolled her eyes. "Yeah, well, if I recall correctly, you were the one saying I didn't need any beauty sleep. Besides, this should be a piece of cake compared to what we've been doing with Griffin Force lately. Silver Mountain is only an hour away, and I think we can help wrap this up."

Sam's face brightened at her words. "All I need is for you two to help me scoop him," he agreed. "Then you're home free. I'll wish you a Merry Christmas and be on my way."

Colt couldn't say no to both of them and didn't really need to be convinced. They would help roll up Jassim, then get back to their holiday plans. Easy day. He leaned forward. "Then I guess you just got yourself a team. Let's go get him."

CHAPTER FOUR

Brenna sat in the backseat, only half-listening as Colt and Sam figured out the best way to head off Jassim and get him to Ottawa. She'd been searching for Nazer for so long, it seemed strange to have another name as the mission target---one that needed to be rescued instead of captured. Her mind was already racing ahead to what contacts she had that she could reach out to and get some more background on Jassim. That was the part of the job she loved---working a problem and finding a solution. Intelligence was all about putting the moving parts together to find that last puzzle piece, and she loved it. She was good at it.

"Do you have a weapons and communications package for us?" she asked Sam when there was a break in their conversation.

"It's in the back of the car." He looked over at Colt

who had raised his eyebrows. "No, I didn't bring it for you specifically. I'm in the communications unit, so I always carry stuff like that for emergencies." He put his hand on the car door. "And we better move out. I don't want Jassim getting too far ahead. He's got at least an hour on us as it is."

Colt got out of the car and went around to the trunk with Sam. Brenna followed, burrowing into her coat as the cold air hit her body. Pulling out her toque and gloves, she slipped them on. With the sun going down, the air was cooling considerably.

Colt hefted a duffel out of Sam's trunk, which would presumably have everything they'd need for weapons as well as SAT phones and laptops. This whole situation was starting to feel like a Griffin Force operation, only they were missing the full team. She looked over at Sam. He was probably only a little bit older than Colt had been when he started with JTF2 and she'd gone off to her intelligence assignment. He was tan, which was unusual for a Canadian at this time of year. It wasn't unrealistic to think he'd recently returned from an assignment overseas. She was glad he'd asked them to help, even though it put their Christmas plans on hold for a bit.

"So, how is Hayes doing?" she asked Sam, taking a small gun and survival pack from the car and leaning a hip against the trunk. "I haven't seen him in a really long time."

Sam glanced over at her as he rearranged the three

duffels and two other equipment packages Colt had left behind. "Same as always. Focused on the team, the units, the assignments. I've never seen a man so driven. There isn't anyone who wouldn't go to battle for him. He's the legend everyone wants to train under."

That's what she remembered of Hayes, too. Some things never changed, and that was comforting, in a way. "Glad to hear it. And good to meet you." She straightened and looked up at the setting sun. They didn't have much time if they wanted to find Jassim before the hitman did. "We'd better go."

Colt appeared at Brenna's side. "Ready?"

"Yeah." She picked up the smaller pack and walked to their car. Opening the passenger-side door, she stowed the bag on the floor and got in.

Colt put the duffel he'd taken from Sam's trunk in their back seat, then got behind the wheel. He handed her a couple of cell phones. "So we can keep in touch with Sam."

She put one in her pocket and the other in the cup holder between them and settled in her seat. "You know, Nazer al-Raimi has been our focus for so long, it's strange to be chasing someone else. Almost like we're cheating on him or something."

Colt chuckled. "Well, Nazer might have a connection to this hit on Jassim, if that makes you feel any better." Colt glanced in his rearview mirror, and Brenna turned around. Sam was two car lengths behind them.

"If Nazer's involved, there's a big picture we're not seeing." Brenna frowned. "He always has a plan to move up in the terrorist power structure. But I guess it could be financial, too."

Colt reached over and took her hand. "Well, the quicker we find Jassim, the faster we can figure out if Nazer's involved or not, and get home for Christmas."

She leaned closer and rested her chin on his shoulder. "Sounds great to me." There was something about being out in the field that always energized her and today was no different. Her senses seemed enhanced somehow, her mind focusing on the intel they had and how that fit into the narrative. Having Colt by her side was an added bonus. He would see the things she didn't. He was a great partner to have.

The kilometers passed quickly and they'd just reached the road that led to Silver Mountain when Brenna noticed some tracks in the snow. A car had skidded out. The sun was nearly gone now, and she shielded her eyes against the last rays. "Colt, a black SUV. There." She pointed toward a small ravine and snowbank on the side of the road.

Colt pulled over, and Sam parked behind them. Brenna was already taking handguns out of the pack at her feet. She handed one to Colt. "Feels like old times, back when we were just starting out."

"Yeah, it does. Be careful," he said, before he leaned in to quickly kiss her.

"You, too." She got out of the car, and slipped on the

small backpack of supplies. Zipping her coat up tight, they cautiously moved toward the SUV, their feet crunching in the snow. The air around them suddenly charged, the silence only broken by cars whizzing by on the freeway. The SUV was a dark spot in the white snow, with both doors hanging open, making it look like a blunted arrow. But was anyone inside?

Sam came up behind them, his gun at the ready. "Let's fan out."

Colt nodded, and they broke off. Brenna went to the right, Colt to the left, and Sam stayed the course. They circled the vehicle, slowly drawing nearer. Once they got close, they could see a body in the snow about four meters in front of the SUV. From the size of him, it looked to be the taller bodyguard she'd spoken to at the airport. But where was Jassim?

Brenna continued her side approach, flanking Sam. She zeroed in on the vehicle. Her senses on high alert, she touched the hood of the SUV. The engine was warm, so it couldn't have skidded out very long ago. Colt and Sam were on either side.

"No one inside," Colt said, looking at the empty seats. "Both bodyguards are deceased, gunshot wounds to the head. Their bodies are in a defensive position outside the car. Looks like they fought back."

"Do you think they've already kidnapped Jassim?" Sam asked, looking in the snow. "I'm not seeing any extra footprints or evidence of a struggle, though."

"There." Brenna pointed just to her right. A small

copse of trees hid a trail clearly showing that someone had walked that way. "Looks like the prince might have escaped."

Just then the snow next to her kicked up as a bullet whizzed by. She instinctively moved for the cover of the trees, and Colt dove beside her. Shots pinged around their position. "Can you see where he's firing from?" she said, her breaths coming fast as adrenaline shot through her.

Colt carefully raised his head to get a better view. "I don't have an angle on him. Sam? You got anything?"

"He's on that little ridge. Up there." Sam glanced behind them, probably seeing exactly what the body-guards had seen before they'd been killed. They were in an area with inadequate cover, leaving them too exposed.

Sam pulled his phone out. "No service up here. If I can make it back to the car, I can call Hayes. With Jassim's security detail murdered, I'm sure we'll get some backup."

"Okay. You get us a few reinforcements, and we'll go after Jassim." Colt motioned toward Brenna with his head. "Let's move. I'll cover you."

Brenna crouched, ready to go on Colt's count. As he fired, she ran to the next tree that would cover her position. Then she popped up and fired toward their shooter while Colt moved next to her. They used that maneuver a few more times, working themselves deeper into the treeline. Brenna glanced at the sky. It was nearly full dark now, which would help hide them from the shooter, but also make it harder to stay on Jassim's trail.

"Can you see any more footprints?" Brenna sucked in a breath and briefly held it to calm her heart rate.

Colt adjusted his stance, keeping his gun ready. He squinted into the encroaching darkness. "They're veering left."

"Then we are, too." She took a flashlight out from her pocket, but didn't turn it on. They walked for another couple of kilometers, staying low and hopefully out of sight. The shooting had finally stopped, but that didn't mean he wasn't still out there. "Do you think we're out of range enough to use a light?"

"I guess we'll find out when you turn it on. Hopefully Sam can get some reinforcements up here quickly, and they'll take the shooter out while we work on tracking down our lost prince. Divide and conquer."

Brenna turned on the flashlight, and when no gunshots sounded near their position, they followed the tracks in the snow, staying aware of their surroundings. The footprints led them down a small valley and Brenna spotted a figure propped against a tree wearing the same blue coat Jassim had at the airport.

"Colt." She inclined her head in the direction of the prince. "There's Jassim. Against that tree at your two o'clock."

They carefully approached him, but he didn't even

stir. Kneeling down at his side, Brenna could see blood oozing from his stomach. "He's hit. And it's bad."

Jassim groaned as Brenna laid him down on the ground. "There's no exit wound." She sat back on her heels. "Do you want to try and get him back to the car? He needs to be in the hospital."

Wood from the tree trunk next to her splintered and ricocheted into the snow at her feet. Colt pulled her down and covered her body with his. "You okay?" he asked in her ear.

"Yeah. I guess Sam's reinforcements haven't gotten here yet." Brenna looked over at Jassim. He hadn't moved from where she'd laid him, and his face was ghostly pale. "No way we can get him back to the car with a shooter on us."

"I think we're going to have to use our winter-survival training to go deeper into the mountain and find a place to hunker down for the night." Colt moved aside, but stayed low. "We've got to give Sam more time to get us some help."

Brenna shifted over until she was beside him. "Okay. I'll cover you." She raised her gun as Colt struggled to get Jassim into a fireman's carry. Jassim was conscious, but seemed in a daze, probably going into shock. They had to get him somewhere safe so they could treat his wound enough to keep him from dying on the mountain.

Once they were set and ready to roll, Brenna kept a

careful watch on the spot where the gun flashes were coming from. "Go!"

Colt moved deep into the trees. He'd only taken ten steps when another shot rang out. Brenna shot back. With only a handgun, they didn't have a chance of hitting the sniper from this distance, but maybe they could fool him as to where exactly they were positioned. She shot again, then followed Colt.

They hiked for nearly an hour, trudging through a stream to hide their tracks, and being careful to stay as far under the cover of trees as they could. Jassim moaned every now and again, but otherwise didn't speak or try to move. When Colt finally stopped walking, he gently set Jassim down underneath a tall tree whose branches had covered the ground enough that there were only a few centimeters of snow.

"Lie on your back with your knees up," Colt told him. "We need to take pressure off your abdomen. I think this is as far as we're going to get tonight."

Brenna looked around. The spot he'd chosen was secluded and on a bit of a rise, so they'd have good tactical position. "What supplies do we have? Anything in your coat pockets?"

"Just what you brought." He reached over and slid the small backpack off her. "Hopefully Sam put a few more items in than just communication equipment that won't work up here." He unzipped the bag and peered inside. "Looks like we're in luck."

Brenna moved closer and poked around the pack.

"Survival shelter, handwarmers, water, energy bars. Thank you, Sam."

"I'll get to it." Colt pulled out the small shovel, then went over to a flat spot and began digging into the snow to make their shelter for the night.

Brenna took one of the water packs and moved toward Jassim. He was watching her, but he seemed dazed and didn't say anything. She sat down next to him and held out the water. "Hey."

"Where am I?" he asked, his voice raspy. His hand shook, and he wasn't able to take more than a sip. She steadied his grasp, then lifted it to his lips so he could get a little more.

"We're on Silver Mountain. Do you remember what happened to you?" she asked quietly. The soft snow and trees surrounding them gave the illusion of safety. Hopefully they could turn it into reality.

"The car's tire blew and we went off the road. The second we got out, someone started shooting." He visibly swallowed at the memory. "I ran."

"You were hit." Brenna motioned toward the wound that was still seeping blood through his coat. "The cold helped you a bit so you didn't bleed out, but stomach wounds are generally serious. We need to get you to a doctor."

"Aren't you the woman from the airport?" Jassim looked at her and furrowed his brow, as if he was trying to place her. "Are you following me? What's really going on?"

"I'm with the Canadian government, sort of, and there's a credible threat on your life. Captain Mitchell and I were asked to help bring you in safely." Brenna looked over at Colt, who was lashing down the shelter. "We were hoping to find you before anything happened."

"Who shot me?" Jassim tried to sit up a little bit to look at his wound, but gasped with pain and sank back.

"We think it's a Russian sniper who works as a mercenary for the highest bidder. Your father's attempt to broker peace in Syria made some powerful enemies." Brenna scanned the perimeter, but all seemed quiet. "We're going to stay here tonight, then hopefully hike out in the morning."

Jassim shivered and turned his face to the darkened sky. "Spend the night here? We'll freeze to death."

Brenna grinned, her gaze going to Colt, who didn't even seem fazed that he was building a snow shelter. Just a month ago he'd been sweltering in a shack on the border of Afghanistan. "Captain Mitchell is highly trained in this sort of thing."

"Are you both in the military, then?" Jassim asked. Gone was the flirtatious man who was a little drunk and much too cocky. The man in front of her now was wounded and scared. He still had that little lost boy look about him, though.

Brenna was glad to see a little color coming back into his cheeks, though his shivers were getting stronger. She reached over to pull a mylar blanket out of the pack. Kneeling down, she draped it over his body and tucked the corners underneath him. "He's military, I'm in intelligence."

Colt walked over to them and stuck the shovel in the snow. He wiped his brow. "All right, let's get you inside," he said to Jassim. "I want you out of sight."

Brenna got on one side of Jassim, and Colt got on the other. They carefully helped him into the small makeshift shelter. Every gasp and groan from him made Brenna's middle twist in sympathy. He was in excruciating pain, but there wasn't much she could do about it. She wished they had another option, but with a stomach wound, and no way to get to a hospital, they needed to keep Jassim as still as possible and control the bleeding. Waiting for other agents to track down the sniper was the best option.

Once they'd gotten him inside the small shelter, Colt took some extra gauze from the pack and made a compress for Jassim's wound. "I'm going to take a look and see what we're dealing with," Colt said, bending over Jassim's chest to unzip his coat.

Jassim could barely nod. Colt went ahead and pushed his coat aside and unbuttoned Jassim's shirt. With practiced efficiency, he put the field dressing on the wound. "I wish Elliot was here," he murmured. Elliot was their Griffin Force medic and was very good at what he did.

"You're doing great." Brenna watched him tie off the ends of the bandage and make sure it would stay put.

Buttoning Jassim's shirt back up, Colt zipped his coat and pulled his hat over his ears. Pulling out the survival sleeping bag, he unfolded it and handed her one end. "Help me get him in this."

They gently pushed and pulled the mylar material over him and once he was inside, the tension in Jassim's face seemed to relax a bit as his body began to warm up.

Within a few minutes, Jassim's breathing evened out and he seemed more comfortable than he had been all night. Hoping he could sleep for a while, Brenna backed out of the shelter and Colt followed. They stayed close by the entrance, just in case he woke up and needed them.

Colt pulled the pack over to rummage through it. He triumphantly held up a small, one-burner stove. "We can light this and get a bit of heat. Maybe even warm up one of the energy bars for a little variety."

Brenna gave a little laugh and shook her head. "Melted energy bars sound terrible, but heat sounds great." She pulled her toque down over her ears and adjusted the mylar blanket over her legs while he lit the burner. Inching closer, she put her gloved hands out toward the tiny flame. "This is cozy."

Colt sat down, his eyes on her. "You did great out there."

She grinned and scooted next to him. How did he always feel so warm? "If you don't count escaping

Nazer's stronghold, this is our first time in the field together."

"And we're killing it." He pulled the burner closer. "The target is safe, we're taking the first watch while we wait for backup. Textbook."

Brenna chuckled at his assessment. He always looked on the bright side. "Well, we still have a Russian sniper hunting for us and we're camping in the dead of a Canadian winter. Not quite textbook."

"Minor details." Colt reached for her hands and pulled off her gloves. Rubbing her fingers between his, he brought them to his lips. "The sniper's probably given up for the night anyway, so that doesn't count against us."

"Let's hope so." His touch sparked a flare of warmth that moved from her hands to her arms and through her middle. Wanting more, she reached up and touched his cheek. The stubble underneath her fingers rubbed against the pad of her thumb and she was unable to resist stroking his jaw down to the cleft in his chin. "I was thinking earlier how we've gone from the extreme heat of Afghanistan to a cold winter. I don't know which I prefer."

"I would choose the winter, so I have an excuse to warm you up." Colt smiled and leaned in, his eyes on her lips. "And once this is over, I promise you, we are going to have an amazing Christmas together with our family, just like we'd planned."

Dipping his head, his mouth touched hers, and the

cold was forgotten as his kiss ignited a fire in her blood that raced through her body. Pressing closer, she put her arms around his neck, letting her hands thread through his hair. He kissed his way along her jaw to the sensitive spot near her ear. Her breaths were coming fast and hard, and she tilted her head to bring him back to her lips.

When they finally broke apart, her heart was pounding in her ribcage as if it were fighting to get free. "I'm feeling a lot warmer now, thank you." She wasn't lying. Her face still felt flushed.

"Bren, I . . ."

But they both stilled when they heard a branch breaking behind them. Quickly putting out the small flame, they both drew their guns and positioned themselves back-to-back. Attuned to the forest around them, Brenna closed her eyes so she could concentrate on listening for any sounds that would give away the position of whomever had found them.

But she quickly opened them when the unmistakable sound of a gun cocked just a few meters in front of them.

CHAPTER FIVE

Colt's entire body hummed with tension. If Jassim made a sound, whoever was in front of them was ready to fire. They'd have their target. He squinted into the trees. All he could see were shadows. Flicking off the gun's safety, the soft *snick* seemed loud in the silence.

"Don't shoot!" A voice whisper-yelled. "It's me, Sam." His looming shape appeared out of the trees closest to them, his hands held out where Colt could see them. He holstered his gun and gave him a rueful look. "Sorry. Didn't mean to scare you. Just staying ready." He crossed the last few feet to their position and crouched next to Brenna, glancing at the shelter. "How's Jassim?"

Colt put the safety back on and lowered the gun. "Not a great idea to sneak up on us like that. We could have killed you." He exhaled, tamping down his annoyance. "He's not great. We did the best we could. What's the situation with our sniper?"

"We've got two operators on the ground tracking him. We picked up his trail three kilometers to the west. I split off to come find you. We're radio silent until check-in at zero one-hundred hours." He looked around, as if the operators or the sniper might appear in the trees.

Which is still a real possibility, Colt thought. *We need to stay ready.*

Sam took off the pack he was carrying and sat down. "It wasn't easy to pick up your trail. I figured you would head for the stream to try and cover your tracks. Even with that, you didn't leave much behind to give away your position. This Russian is relentless, though. He's not going to give up easily."

"Is there a plan?" Brenna stood and brushed snow off of her bottom.

"I secured a safehouse for us, but it's about two kilometers north of this location." He glanced at the tent. "With that storm rolling in, we need a solid shelter. We'll have to get Jassim up."

"He probably won't have his wound reopened if both of us carry him." Colt stood and started toward the tent. "We'll need to get him to a doctor soon."

Sam followed, tugging his hat down. "I know. But we can't take the chance of bringing him out in the open with the sniper so close. Best to take cover at the safehouse until the sniper is out of the picture and Jassim can be transported."

"Okay, let's do this." Colt went into the shelter first, crawling over to Jassim. He hated to move the man, but there wasn't anything else they could do with a storm coming. Time was running out, and they needed to get him to a better shelter or exposure to the elements would kill him before the bullet wound. Colt maneuvered around to his shoulders, and Sam stayed near his feet. They kept him in the survival sleeping bag for warmth. He was going to need every bit he could get.

Jassim groaned as they moved him as carefully as possible and took him back outside. His skin was turning a bit gray, and Colt's concern ratcheted up. The man couldn't afford to lose much more blood.

Once they'd laid him down on a small patch of ground that wasn't completely snow-covered, Sam stood watch while Colt and Brenna quickly took down the shelter and hid any trace that their group had stopped here. They worked seamlessly together, their movements in sync as they always had been. She seemed to know exactly what needed to be done before he could point it out. One more connection between them that he'd been able to count on when they'd first dated years ago. After working without that bond for so long, he knew now how rare it was and felt lucky they still had it.

When everything was packed and their presence there untraceable, they moved up the ridge. Colt and Sam had Jassim between them in a modified two-handed seat carry while Brenna kept an eye out for any unwanted shooters. They went as fast as they could, but each step was starting to feel heavier, as if Colt's feet were filling up with frozen lead. The cold had permeated his boots, and if not for the now-cooling foot warmers, he was sure they wouldn't be more than blocks of ice. He watched Brenna. She had to be just as cold and hungry as he was, but she never complained. He marveled at her ability to adapt to any situation. No wonder she'd received one of the most dangerous assignments with Griffin Force. She was just that good.

"How much farther?" Colt asked. Jassim's face was getting progressively more gray. He needed to rest. Preferably in a hospital, but definitely not out in the elements on a cold, Canadian night in the middle of winter.

"It's up ahead. Half a kilometer, if that. You can see the outline just through those trees." Sam was breathing heavy, but the sight of the cabin seemed to help him rally. None of them said anything else as they focused on their objective. Time seemed to be slowing down with each step, though it probably only took another twenty minutes. They finally made it to the door and waited while Brenna followed Sam's directions and got the key from a loose board near the front of the porch. It took a bit of maneuvering to get Jassim through the door without jostling him too much. Once they got inside, Brenna turned on her flashlight and led the way to the kitchen table.

"We need to get a look at that wound." Brenna motioned for them to put Jassim on the farmhouse table made of smooth wooden planks. It easily could have passed for something out of a pioneer museum.

Sam took off his gloves and started to unzip Jassim's coat. "I brought a medical kit. You two go secure the perimeter."

Colt nodded and turned to Brenna, silently communicating as they both took stock of the small cabin. It wouldn't take long to secure the place. He started at the door and she took the windows. The curtains were a thick burlap to keep out the cold, which would be helpful in hiding their presence. The door locks were serviceable, but if someone really wanted to get in, they wouldn't be hard to break. Colt checked his ammunition. Hopefully this wouldn't come to a standoff. They didn't have enough firepower to last long.

Brenna appeared at his side. "There's a kerosene heater in the corner. Looks like it's in good condition." She looked up at him. "After being in Afghanistan for so long, I forgot what winter really feels like."

He grinned. "Are you saying your blood got thin?"

"Or Canada got colder." She shivered.

Colt wanted to draw her close and warm her up with kisses, but a kerosene heater would have to do for the moment. He glanced over to the corner. "Let's get that heater going."

Colt carefully worked with the wick and kerosene, checking and double-checking before he lit it. The flame was a welcome sight. He brought the heater over to the table where Sam and Brenna were on either side of Jassim. Sam had a medical field kit open next to him and was just finishing packing Jassim's stomach wound.

He looked over at Colt, his eyes grim. "I got the bullet, but I can't tell how much internal damage there is. We've got to get him to a hospital sooner rather than later."

Colt looked down at Jassim, deathly pale and still. "We can't move him in this condition. That'd finish him off for sure."

"The second I get the all clear, I'll see if I can get an AirMed helicopter up here." Sam put one more gauze bandage over the wound to keep the packing in place.

Brenna's pained expression said everything Colt was thinking. They were doing all they could for Jassim, but it might not be enough.

She moved to the chair near the small kitchen counter, nearest the heater. Putting out her hands, she rubbed them together and then faced them toward the heat. "I never thought I'd feel my fingers again," she said with a sigh. "That heat is heavenly."

Colt joined her, clasping her hand in between his. "Let me help."

The longer they stood in front of the heater, the more her muscles began to relax. The room was beginning to get warmer for all of them. Sam pulled up the blanket over Jassim and glanced over at them. "Thanks for all you two did today."

"I'm glad we were there." Colt leaned closer to the table, but kept Brenna's hand in his. "Is there any more intel about Jassim and what's really going on? This has to be about more than manipulating his father to stop providing humanitarian aid or brokering peace in Syria."

Sam rubbed the back of his neck and watched Jassim for a moment before turning to face Colt and Brenna directly. "Not that there needs to be another reason, but Jassim does have enemies of his own. He's been vocal against his father's attempts to broker peace in Syria. He feels that Russia has meddled in the Syrian civil war for their own gain, and that there should be a coalition of Middle Eastern governments to stand against them. Jassim's stances on foreign policy issues are considered radical, and he's not well-liked in any government circles. That could be part of the reasoning behind the hit."

"So do you think Russia just wants to take Jassim out of the equation, then?" Brenna asked. "Or is this more about his father's position?"

Sam pulled up a chair next to them and sat. He let

out a long exhale, the corners of his mouth turning down in a frown. "I don't know. The war in Syria is a delicate situation and there are a lot of groups trying to take advantage of the chaos. Nazer could very well be one of them. The assassination of a Kuwaiti emir's son would definitely cause unrest in the region, and that's part of his M.O. The chaos would attract him, cover his attempts to make inroads with any terrorist groups nearby. His name *has* been mentioned a couple of times on the terrorist channels we monitor and we've been trying to validate what our intelligence agencies have picked up, but aren't having much luck so far."

"Yeah, we know all about Nazer's M.O. I feel like I know that guy better than I know myself sometimes." Colt's gaze flicked to Brenna. She'd never flinched at Nazer's name being mentioned, but it got under his skin every time, with all he'd put them through. He touched the burn on his arm that he'd received when Nazer had captured him. All of their lives had been changed by Nazer al-Raimi, and Colt would do anything to see the man captured and put away.

Jassim started to stir, so all three of them stood and went to his side. His head began to thrash from side to side.

"Shh, you're safe now," Brenna told him, carefully putting her hand on his shoulder. "Just rest."

He opened his eyes and stared at her. He began to speak, but it was in Arabic. Brenna leaned in closer, her brow furrowing as she listened to his raspy words.

She spoke back to him in his native tongue, and he shook his head violently. Reaching out, he grasped her arm and pulled her against him. His voice wavered, but he pleaded with her, then began to shout as loud as his hoarse voice would allow.

Colt stepped up and put himself between her and Jassim. "What's he saying?"

Brenna turned worried eyes to him. "He wants to talk to his father right away. Lives depend on it." She looked back at Jassim. "He says that he has to confess before he dies, or the souls of thousands will be on his head."

"Souls of thousands?" Colt asked. "Does he mean some sort of terrorist attack?"

"M-many will die." Jassim whispered, switching to English, his eyes drifting closed. "I must speak to my father before they're all dead."

Colt rubbed a hand over his face and turned his head in Sam's direction. Just when he thought the situation couldn't get any worse. "If the Russian is as good as we think he is, we can't use the SAT phone without giving away our position. That would lead him right to us."

After a small pause, Sam reached into the backpack and took out the SAT phone. "I only see one option here," he said, his words solemn.

A shiver of foreboding raced through Colt. Their choices were dwindling fast. And there was something bigger here that was just waiting to pounce on them.

Meeting Brenna's eyes, he could see she felt it, too. But there wasn't any fear. She was resolute. Ready.

And so was he.

CHAPTER SIX

Brenna watched them get set up for Jassim's phone call to his father using the emir's private line. Sam was making the right decision, but it still put them all in danger. The SAT phone could only be used for ten minutes or less before they would be compromised and have to move. Only, they couldn't move. Jassim wasn't in any condition to go anywhere and there was a real chance he still might die no matter what they did.

Once Sam had the emir on the line, he handed the bulky SAT phone to Jassim. He shakily took it in his hand, pulling it to his chest and taking a deep breath. A sheen of tears appeared in his eyes, and Brenna's heart ached for him. He was afraid. Looking death in the face was a life-changing experience. She'd been there herself and didn't wish that on anyone.

Putting the phone to his ear, he cleared his throat.

"Father." Jassim was quiet for a moment while he listened, then shook his head. "Listen to me. I need to tell you something."

He was speaking in English, and his speech was more formal than Brenna expected. How big was the breach between them?

Jassim looked at her before turning his face away. "Father." He swallowed. "I'm sorry. I wish I could take back what I've done. I was foolish and thought I was showing strength, but now I see that I've only weakened your position."

Sam and Colt were watching Jassim carefully as well. The three of them seemed to be held motionless by the scene unfolding in front of them. What had he done?

Coughing, it took Jassim several seconds to catch his breath. When he did, he spoke quickly. "I made a deal with a faction of Hurras al-Din to send guns and ammunition to Syria mixed in with your humanitarian shipments. I paid off the officials receiving the relief crates to put the weapons to the side." He coughed again. "I'm so sorry. I wanted to stand up to the Russians, to show our strength. To help those fighting oppression."

Brenna held her breath. What kind of weapons were in those crates? The Hurras al-Din was affiliated with al-Qaeda and were the stronghold in Syria for rebuilding what leverage al-Qaeda had there. If they were given a large shipment of arms, that could turn the tide in the war on terror and give men like Nazer an advantage. And there was no doubt Nazer would be involved in a deal like that. She exhaled slowly and her eyes met Colt's. His jaw was clenched tight and he looked as concerned as she felt.

Jassim listened carefully to whatever his father was saying, but wasn't in a hurry to end the call. Brenna didn't blame him. If she thought she was dying, and this might be the last time she talked to her father, she wouldn't want to rush. But Sam was checking his watch. They only had a few more minutes before they'd be compromised. Motioning for Jassim to wrap it up, they waited another minute. Jassim told his father he loved him, then hung up.

"It's done." He slowly handed the phone back to Sam and wilted before their eyes, pulling in on himself, as if he'd used up all his strength. He didn't have much longer. They needed to get out of here.

"We've got to get him to a hospital," Brenna whispered. She wasn't used to feeling helpless. Standing here and watching Jassim die would haunt her for the rest of her life. She wanted to do something.

"I know." Colt gripped the edge of the table and leaned over Jassim. "Is Nazer involved in the deal you made with the Hurras al-Din?"

Jassim let his head fall to one side and closed his eyes, as if he knew death was near and was readying himself for it. "Nazer is aware of the situation in Syria."

"But is he part of this deal?" Colt pressed.

"I don't want my last words to be about Nazer al-Raimi." Jassim slowly turned his head to face Colt, his words measured and deliberate. "I want to die in peace."

Colt shook his head. "There will be no peace as long as Nazer is free. If you have information about where he is or what his plans are, help us capture him. Then, if the worst happens, your conscience will be clear." Colt pinned Jassim with his gaze. "Help us."

The command hung in the air of the cabin as the two men faced off. Neither of them blinked as the seconds ticked by.

"I don't know many details." Jassim couldn't hold back a cough and finally turned away. "Nazer has strongholds near the Turkish border. The oil fields are of interest to him." He closed his eyes again. "That's all I have to say."

"We need to know more. All of it." Colt touched his shoulder, but Jassim didn't respond. "Please. Tell us all you can. I'll protect you. Nazer has killed and hurt so many people. We need your help to bring him in."

Jassim ignored Colt and kept his eyes closed. He was giving up. Could they keep him alive much longer? She didn't think so.

Brenna needed to think. There had to be a way out of this. Something they could do. She stepped away from the table and went to the corner of the kitchen. Colt followed.

He stopped in front of her, folding his arms before

leaning his hip against the cupboard. She looked up at his familiar face, glad he was there.

"Do you think Nazer is using the Hurras al-Din to get the weapons and take over the oil field? The money he could get on the black market for that oil would fund his operations for years to come." Brenna kept her voice down, but couldn't hide the worry in it. They'd been chasing Nazer and trying to shut down all his financing for so long. It would be a big blow if he got hold of an oil field.

"That's what I was thinking. Syria is in so much turmoil, he could turn it to his advantage if he had enough weapons. Jassim's 'show of strength' would be the perfect opportunity. Not to mention if it ever came out that weapons were smuggled in with humanitarian supplies, it would embarrass the emir and possibly cripple any future diplomatic overtures." He glanced at Jassim. "I wish he would trust us with all he knows. In case anything happens."

"He won't last much longer." Brenna twisted her wrist so she could see the time on her watch. "Sam's team should be checking in soon. I feel like I should be doing something instead of just waiting to be found." She pointed behind her. "I saw a roll of barbed wire outside. Maybe we could set some perimeter traps. Might buy us some time if the Russian finds the cabin."

"That's not a bad idea. We'd need some gloves and wire cutters." Colt looked at the door and back at Jassim. "Working in Special Ops has helped my patience levels and adapting in the field, but in situations like this, it's still hard not to want to get out there and get it done."

"Yeah." She took his hand and squeezed his fingers. "I know what you mean."

They walked back to Sam who was at the sink, filling a bowl with cool water. "He's running a fever, and I already gave him the meds I had in the kit that would bring it down. I'm going to do what I can with this." He motioned to the cloth in the water.

"We're going to set some perimeter traps." Brenna took the bowl from him and set it near Jassim's hip.

"Don't you think we should all stay together? If the Russian finds us, I'd rather have all three of us right here for the firefight." Sam immersed the cloth he had and wrung it out before he bathed Jassim's face.

His eyelids fluttered, and he murmured some Arabic that sounded like he was asking for his mother. Not a good sign. Brenna looked over at Sam and took the cloth from him. She pressed it to Jassim's neck, listening closely to what he was whispering. "Change is coming," he said, with his next breath. "I'm sorry. Please don't leave me."

He was getting agitated, so Brenna took his hand. "I'm here, Jassim. I will keep you safe." He quieted and seemed to relax a bit. She let go to dip the cloth one more time, wringing it out before she laid it on his head. "Tell me about the change that is coming."

"We're going to fight." He sighed deeply. "Nazer will

be at the meeting with Abu al-Masri and Tariq. They will discuss all the targets."

Brenna stared at Jassim. Did he just say what she thought he said? "When is the meeting?" Jassim didn't respond, so she bent down close to his ear. "Jassim! When is the meeting?"

Colt appeared at her side. "What's going on? What is he saying?"

"There's a meeting between Nazer, Abu al-Masri, and Tariq Hammam, but he didn't say when. If we can get intel on his exact location, we could finally capture him." Excitement was building in Brenna. This was the break they'd been waiting for. Knowing Nazer's location in advance was so extremely rare since he moved constantly.

Colt looked down at Jassim and shook his head. "We need details to make sure it's not just the fever talking."

Brenna leaned down to speak close to Jassim's ear again. "Jassim, you must tell me. Where is the meeting?"

The wounded man twitched restlessly, his face grimacing in pain. "Stop the meeting. Stop the guns," he whispered in Arabic.

Brenna was worried he was slipping away. She put her hand on his forearm, squeezing it gently. "I want to help you stop the meeting, Jassim," she told him. "Where is it taking place? You have to help me."

"You must hurry. In Idlib. On Thursday." Jassim let

out a long breath, and the room was silent. Had he stopped breathing? Alarmed, Brenna laid her head on his chest. His heartbeat was still there under her ear. Thready, but still beating. Relieved, she straightened and looked up at Colt.

"We've got to get out of here and alert Julian that Nazer's going to be in Syria." This was it. She could feel it. Knowing where Nazer was going would give them the element of surprise. He wouldn't expect them to have his location and that would be to their advantage. They'd have a real chance of capturing him.

Colt looked pained. "We don't have enough time left on the SAT phone before it's traceable. If we risk a call to Julian, our position is compromised. But if we don't, we could risk losing our window to catch Nazer."

"We've got to take the risk in getting a call out. This is too important," Brenna told him.

But before he could answer, the window near the door shattered. Colt, Brenna, and Sam all dove for cover.

The Russian had found them.

CHAPTER SEVEN

Colt quickly pulled his gun and got into position near the broken window. Peeking around the edge, he scanned the trees, but the moonlight wasn't revealing the sniper's location. Another shot rang out, hitting the corner of the house about two meters away from Colt. The wide miss told Colt that the gunman no longer had a clean shot. He was going to need to get closer and that's when Colt would strike.

Keeping his eyes glued to the treeline, Colt saw the gunman make his move. He ran in a zigzag pattern, working his way to the cabin a little at a time. Colt fired, kicking up some snow right on the man's heels. The sniper briefly looked over at him, then took cover.

Brenna appeared at Colt's side. "Get anything?" Her gun was out and ready.

"I don't have a good angle from here. He's staying

low and moving in." Colt's gaze skimmed over the cabin. The windows were small and inadequate for what they were facing. "I've got to get up on the roof so I can get eyes on him."

Concern flickered through her eyes, but she agreed. "I'll cover you." Brenna touched his cheek and gave him a quick kiss. "Stay safe."

"You, too." He turned and picked up the rifle Sam had brought with him. Brenna took over his position at the window. "Stay close to Jassim," he instructed Sam as he passed. Sam nodded, busy trying to push the table into a more secure position in the corner of the room.

After he carefully eased the back door of the cabin open, Colt slipped out. With the rifle slung over his back, he used a piece of a tree trunk that was waiting to be split, to boost himself up on the roof. He grabbed the edge and pulled his body onto the snow-covered housetop. With a quick scan of his surroundings, Colt kept low, while he belly-crawled up to the ridgeline of the cabin. Getting his rifle ready, he looked through the scope. No sign of the sniper. Settling in, he swept the area. The guy couldn't have gone far. He'd show himself soon enough.

A flash in the snow appeared through the darkness as the sniper took aim at the cabin again. The sound of glass splintering echoed over the snow, and Colt heard Brenna returning fire. *That's my girl*, he thought with a grin.

The gunman quickly retreated before Colt could set

up his shot. This was going to be more like a siege than a hit unless the gunman showed his face for longer than a half second. They needed to lure him out.

Colt heard the front door to the cabin open, and Brenna's light tread sounded across the small porch as she ran to the right of the cabin. His heart leapt into his throat. She must have come to the same realization he had about drawing the gunman closer. But she was using herself as bait!

He wanted to look for her, see for himself that she'd made it to a safe spot, but he focused on where he'd last seen the sniper. The best way to keep her safe was to do his job. The sniper poked his head up and quickly squeezed off two shots before he disappeared again. Colt heard a soft thud in the snow and hoped with everything he had that Brenna hadn't been hit. The thud he'd heard was only her finding some cover.

Keeping a careful watch, Colt kept his scope trained on where the shots had come from. The sniper finally showed himself, raising his head up, then his chest, trying to see if he'd hit his target. It was enough of a window that Colt had a clear shot. He held his breath and took it.

The sniper went down with a loud groan.

Brenna appeared in front of the cabin and started moving toward the sniper. Her gun was at the ready. *Wait*, he wanted to yell, but instead, he scrambled off the roof as quickly as he could so he could give her some backup. Once he was back on the ground, Colt jogged toward the sniper's last position, coming at it from the opposite side of where Brenna was approaching. If the gunman was still alive, or tried anything, they'd have him in their crossfire.

When they both rounded the large rock the sniper had been hiding behind, the bright moonlight illuminated his body on the ground, blood staining the snow underneath him. His rifle had skidded away on some ice. When the gunman saw them, though, he grimaced and reached for a combat knife in his boot. He wasn't giving up.

"Drop it," Brenna barked out, her voice breaking the silence. She pointed her gun at his chest. "Now."

"*Nyet.*" The sniper shakily stood, using the rock behind him as leverage. His shoulder wound oozed dark blood down his parka. He pointed his blade at them, motioning Colt forward. "Let's finish this."

That sounded good to Colt. He took two steps forward, with Brenna at his side, slightly behind him. They moved as a unit, ready for anything. When they were three meters away, Colt raised his gun. "Put the knife down. I'd rather not shoot you again."

The gunman let out a primal scream and ran toward Colt, the knife in his hand pointed right at Colt's stomach. But a gunshot rang out before the sniper had taken more than three steps. He yelled loudly as he went down for the second time. Brenna lowered her gun and reached his side first to kick his knife out of the way. Colt pinned the sniper on the ground and zip tied his hands behind his back. With a gunshot wound in both shoulders, he could hardly contain a howl of pain at the movement. Once he was subdued, Colt got him to his feet. Brenna picked up the guy's gun and backpack. It was over.

They took him inside. Sam had been able to position Jassim in the corner, still on the table, but behind a mattress that offered some protection. His eyes grew round when they entered the cabin. "You got him."

"We got him," Colt confirmed. He sat the sniper in the chair nearest the door. "Let's call this in. Now that we're not being hunted, we can request an air rescue for Jassim. And probably him, too." He leaned down and looked at the wounds in the gunman's shoulder. "Yeah, definitely him, too. Shoulder wounds can be nasty."

The Russian glared at Colt, his jaw clenched. "They'll never get here in time," he gritted out from between his teeth.

"You're going to be fine." Brenna assured him. "We want you around for questioning."

"I meant him." The sniper jerked his head toward Jassim, whose breaths were shallow and slow. "He's nearly dead already."

Colt glanced at Jassim. His chest was still rising, so they had a chance. "Don't collect your bounty money just yet. Jassim's a fighter."

The gunman gave a cruel laugh. "I would have done

it for free." He spit blood on the floor. "The emir and his son have no honor, and they will pay for that."

"Not if we can help it." Sam walked into the kitchen and got on his radio. It didn't take long before a rescue helo was on its way. "Ten minutes out," he said, as he rejoined them. "And our agents were located. Wounded, but not life-threatening." He turned to the sniper. "You've failed on every front."

The Russian smirked at Sam before turning his gaze on Jassim who was deathly still. "We shall see."

"I'd be more worried about your own future," Brenna put in. Colt's attention focused on her as she walked past them to the broken window and looked up into the darkened sky. Pulling on her gloves, she kept her face carefully blank, the practiced look of every intelligence agent as they compartmentalized their feelings.

Colt went to her side, the cold air from the broken window hitting him full in the face. "Hey," he said, watching her carefully. "You okay?"

She twisted around to catch his eye. "I'm fine." But the flat look she gave him said that wasn't quite true.

He reached out and rubbed a hand over her shoulder. "I wish you could have given me a heads up you were planning to use yourself as bait."

"We had to have a distraction. I took care of that, and you took care of him. Piece of cake." She smiled up at him, the blank look slipping away to reveal the real Brenna. The woman he loved. His heart thudded in his chest. She was so confident in her abilities, and so easygoing about doing whatever it took to get the job done. That quality was one of the things he loved about her, though it did scare him sometimes when she put herself in harm's way.

He looked at his watch. It was nearly two in the morning. "It's Christmas." He pulled her into the crook of his arm. "Not quite what I had imagined when we talked about coming home for the holidays."

She surveyed the men in the room. "Yeah, I wasn't expecting to spend Christmas with a Russian mercenary, a Kuwaiti prince, and a Canadian operator in a cabin in the woods. But you did keep part of your promise. We *are* together."

"Always," he murmured and kissed her temple. Ever since they'd found each other again, he hadn't wanted to leave her side. They'd been apart long enough. "And there's still plenty of Christmas day left. I plan to keep every part of my promise to spend Christmas with both of our families, too."

"I'd like that." She closed her eyes for a moment, then opened them, weariness in every line of her face and body. They both needed some rest, but there was still a lot to do. The second he could, however, he was going to make sure she got some sleep.

Brenna reluctantly moved out of his arms just as they heard the helo's low *thwump thwump*. "We should probably brief Julian about Nazer's meeting in Syria, ASAP."

Colt agreed and took her hand as they walked to Sam's side. He was standing guard over Jassim whose breathing was labored, but still regular. That was a miracle in itself.

"Just hang on," Colt said softly to him. They'd come this far. He had to pull through.

Brenna took the SAT phone and headed for the door. Medical personnel arrived, pulling a rescue basket behind them and a large medical bag. Colt watched her let them in before she walked outside. Part of him wanted to be there when she updated Julian on the intel they had about Nazer being in Syria. Their team leader would be ecstatic about that lead.

Colt stood back as the rescue team readied both Jassim and the Russian for transport. CSIS agents also arrived, and soon the small cabin was filled to capacity. Colt kept an eye on the Russian until he was handed off to the authorities who would oversee his medical care, and then his questioning. Once he was taken away, Colt went to find Brenna.

She finished the call just as he reached her side, and he could feel some tension rolling off of her. "Julian is going to see if they can get drone or satellite surveillance on the meeting place Jassim gave us. The whole team is on their way to Syria, but we have the choice to stay here or join them." Brenna looked up at him and tilted her head, her gaze unreadable.

"We've been chasing him for so long," Colt said, his mind racing with the options in front of him and what each one meant. "I thought I'd want to be there when he was captured. Payback for what he did to us in Afghanistan." Colt moved closer to Brenna, thinking of all they'd suffered the last time they'd been so close to capturing Nazer.

"I'm ready to fly out of here with you and head to Syria, if that's what you want." She touched his jaw, rubbing her palm along the stubble. "I know what it means to you to finish a job. Especially this one."

"But it's more important to me to keep my promises." He bent and kissed her, his hand going to the nape of her neck to nudge her closer. She seemed to melt in his arms, pressing into his body, her warmth igniting the sparks that even a Canadian winter couldn't squelch. He pulled back slightly. "Let's stay. Let's spend Christmas here just like we planned. The team will take care of Nazer."

"You never fail to surprise me." She smiled and gave him one more quick kiss. "Let's go see your family."

CHAPTER EIGHT

Brenna walked outside the cabin and took a deep breath. The moon glinted off the snow, making the red parkas of the law enforcement officers who were swarming up the hill look like shadowy fire bees returning to their hive. It was over. The cavalry was here.

Colt joined her, and Sam wasn't far behind, following the rescue team carrying Jassim's stretcher. "I'll keep you updated on the situation," Sam said as they passed.

One of the medics on the rescue team was holding up an IV bag. They all started walking faster the moment the group cleared the trees, working to get to the clearing where the helo was waiting for them.

Colt put his arm around her waist. "You okay?"

"Yeah." Brenna looked down at her coat covered in

dirt and blood. "Should we start hiking back to the car? Or do you have something you still need to do here?"

"Nope, I'm ready to go." He took her hand, but stopped to watch the helo take off. "I hope Jassim makes it."

"Me, too." She started walking down the hill, leaving the cabin behind.

They walked back the way they'd come. The brightness of the moon was less of a liability now they weren't being chased. The quiet of the trees settled over her, calming the adrenaline that had been flowing through her veins for the past several hours. Her head felt heavy, and at that moment, she wished for a pillow and bed nearby. What a night it had been. And they hadn't even been on Canadian soil for a full twenty-four hours.

"Do you regret deciding to stay here instead of heading to Syria?" she asked Colt, glancing at his face. He was yawning, the dark circles under his eyes attesting to his own exhaustion.

"Not for one second." He squeezed her fingers. "Doesn't feel much different than if we'd been with the team, though, with everything we've been through tonight. Hopefully Julian got the drop on Nazer."

"Do you ever think about what comes next?" A little tremor of nervousness went through her. She'd been wanting to ask this question for a while now, but the timing hadn't ever seemed right before.

"Hopefully a big Christmas dinner." Colt grinned and tugged her closer to him.

"I mean after we catch Nazer. What's your plan for after?" She stopped and pulled him around to face her. She needed to see his expression when he answered.

His eyebrows furrowed and he searched her eyes. "I imagine we'll just move to the next bad guy on the list. There are plenty to take down to keep the world safe. Are you thinking you want to get out of the field?" His hands slid up her arms and cupped her shoulders. "Is that what you're trying to say?"

"No." She exhaled, her breath crystallizing in the cold. "I feel like I was made to do this kind of work. But we need to be on the same page, especially when it comes to the future."

He pulled her in for a hug. "We're partners---on and off the field. That's my plan. If that ever changes, you'll be the first one I talk to about it." Drawing back, he slid his thumb over her jaw and bent to kiss her. His lips were warm, and she pressed closer, reveling in the moment. He'd said exactly what she was hoping he would.

But tingles of cold were sweeping over every nerve ending in her body and she shivered. "I think I'm turning into a block of ice."

"It's like Canada prepared a special welcome home for us." He took her hand, and they started moving toward the car. It seemed like a lifetime since they'd gotten out of the warmth of their little four-door to search for Jassim.

Once Colt got the car started, he turned the heat on full blast. Brenna took off her gloves and put her fingers in front of the vent, rubbing them together. "Where are we going?"

"I thought we'd drive to my mom's. The sun should be up by the time we get there." Colt turned onto the freeway.

"Won't it be a bit early for visitors?" Brenna cupped her hands and blew into them. Her fingers were finally starting to warm up.

"I'm not a visitor. I'm her only son." Colt smiled, as if he was remembering something he'd forgotten. "She's usually up at the crack of dawn every morning."

"Like you." Brenna nudged his shoulder. "Must be a family thing."

The cell phone in Colt's pocket buzzed. He took it out and handed it to Brenna. She accepted the call and put it on speaker. "Colt Mitchell." It was the unmistakable voice of Colonel Hayes.

"Sir." Colt straightened in his seat. He glanced at the phone. "Good to hear from you."

"Glad you could answer. From what I'm hearing, you had some close calls." Hayes cleared his throat. "Thanks for putting yourself on the line today. You and Ms. Wilson averted an international crisis."

"You can always count on us, sir." Colt said, smiling

at Brenna, his eyes warm. It was nice to be recognized as a team.

"Come see me while you're in town. I've heard some stories about you and Griffin Force that sound pretty unbelievable, but since you were trained by the best, I'm sure they're all true." Hayes chuckled. "I'd like to buy you a drink and hear them straight from you. And bring Ms. Wilson with you."

"Yes, sir. We'll be in touch," Colt said. After their goodbyes, they ended the call.

"That was nice of him," Brenna said, leaning back against the headrest. "I remember you saying what a hard-nosed commander he was."

"I have no doubt he still is. He taught me everything I know. And he does love a good war story. If we have time, I'd love to see him and catch up." Colt exited and turned into a residential area. "Almost there."

A prickle of nervousness stabbed Brenna's chest. What if his mom was sleeping? What if she didn't like unexpected guests coming along with her son?

Colt glanced over at her and shook his head. "Trust me." He pulled into the driveway of a two-story home with a wide porch. Colt put the car in park and turned it off before he twisted in his seat. He gently captured her chin with his thumb and forefinger and ducked his head to look her in the eyes. "She. Will. Love. You."

Brenna exhaled. "I hope you're right."

They got out of the car and went up to the front door. Colt rapped on it, and they waited, Brenna's heart pounding as hard as it had the day she infiltrated Nazer's compound. She wished she wasn't standing here after being up all night, rumpled, bloody from tending to a wounded man and dirty from tramping all over a mountain. She had always hoped to make a good impression when she met Colt's family. This wasn't it.

A woman wearing sweats and an oversized sweat-shirt that said 'Don't Mess With Me I'm a Special Forces Mom' with the JTF2 insignia in the corner stood in the doorway. She was drying her hands on a dishtowel, but when she saw Colt, she dropped it. Her hands went to her mouth, and she let out a little cry before she launched herself into his arms.

"Is it really you?" she asked, breathlessly as she hugged him tight. "My imagination hasn't conjured you?"

"It's really me." Colt lifted her off her feet and swung her around. "I've come home for Christmas."

She pulled back and put her hand to his face. "I've missed you so much." Her eyes were wet with tears. "I was just wondering to myself where you were and if you would be able to have any sort of Christmas this year."

"Good to see you, son." Colt's dad came into the living room and made it a group hug with his wife and Colt. "Did I hear you're staying for Christmas?"

"Yeah." Colt drew her forward. "And I brought Brenna with me."

Brenna looked between his parents, putting on her best smile. "I hope you don't mind."

"Not at all! We have plenty of room." Colt's mom walked over and drew her into a hug as well. "I'm so happy you're here. But you look frozen. Take off your parka and wet things, then come into the kitchen and let me warm you up."

Colt and Brenna both took off their outerwear, then let his mom lead the way. They all dutifully followed behind her, as if she were a commanding officer. Once they had crowded into the kitchen, she shooed them toward the stools. "I just took a batch of cinnamon rolls out of the oven, so you can start with them. I'll make some eggs and bacon."

Colt snagged a cinnamon roll from the cooling rack on the counter and took a bite, then sat down with a sigh of pure pleasure. "I've missed your cooking, Mom. I never knew how much until this very moment."

Brenna smiled. Colt did love a home-cooked meal, and that didn't happen very often with their schedule.

Colt's mom looked up when a teenaged girl entered the room. "Did we wake you up, Em?"

"Sorry, princess." Colt turned to look at her, and her sleepy eyes widened.

"Colt! You're home!" She ran and hugged her brother. "I didn't dare wish you'd be here for Christmas this year."

Brenna's eyes misted over watching the siblings

embrace. Coming here had been the right call. They should have come sooner.

Before long, they were all sitting down to a breakfast of bacon and eggs, laughing and talking as they caught up. Colt even gave them a watered-down version of how they'd found each other on an op in Afghanistan. Colt's mother kept glancing at her, and Brenna couldn't tell what her looks meant. Was she happy about them meeting up again? Worried?

Once the breakfast was over and the dishes done, Colt's mother touched Brenna's arm. "I bet you'd like to clean up. Let me show you the guest room."

Colt wiped his hands on a dishtowel. "Is my old room still available for me?"

"It's almost exactly the same way you left it." Emily rolled her eyes. "Practically a shrine."

Colt's mom laughed and waved a hand. "Oh, that's not true. I merely wanted to be ready for something like this.

Brenna liked her. She was so down-to-earth. Just like Colt.

She followed Colt's mom down the hall to a room at the very end. "Jack brought your suitcases in from the car while you were finishing off your meal. There are fresh towels in the towel closet near the vanity. Let me know if you need anything else."

"Thanks, Mrs. Mitchell," Brenna said with a warm smile.

"Call me Nora. I hope we'll be friends." She reached

out and squeezed Brenna's shoulder. "I'm so happy to meet you. Colt mentioned you in nearly every email, letter, and phone call before you two broke up. And he was so quiet after you left, right before he was deployed. I always thought you owned a piece of his heart. I'm so glad you found each other again."

Brenna swallowed, tears pricking the back of her throat. "I'm glad, too. Colt has always had a special place in my life."

Nora hugged her again. "It's so wonderful to have you two here for Christmas."

Brenna watched Nora walk away before she went into the guest room and shut the door. Colt was right. She'd had no reason to worry. His mother couldn't have been more welcoming. She moved over to the bed where her suitcase was and unzipped it. Pulling out clean clothes, she wasted no time getting undressed and into the shower. Hot water had never felt so good. Once she was clean and in fresh clothing, she joined the family back in the family room. They were all sitting on the sofa, just chatting. It was as if they didn't want to miss a moment of the time they had together.

Colt made room on the sofa next to him and she sat down. He was freshly showered as well. Sitting so close, she could smell the spice of his aftershave, combined with the warmth of his body. She could hardly resist snuggling into his side.

"Do you guys want to go tobogganing?" Emily asked. "The old sled hill isn't far."

Colt looked down at Brenna, a knowing glint in his eye. With the night they'd had, being chased by a Russian sniper over a mountain in freezing temperatures, climbing a sledding hill didn't sound like that much fun right now. The corners of his mouth turned up in a smile. "Maybe tomorrow, Em. We're still getting used to the Canadian weather, so we'd like to stay inside, where it's warm."

Emily shook her head. "You've gone soft. It's only minus four outside. That's practically spring temperatures!"

Colt chuckled. "Well, when you've been in Afghanistan for the last six months, sweating it out in the heat and humidity, this is a big change."

"I can imagine," his mom said with a nod. "So this is the perfect time to revisit our family Yahtzee championship."

"You have a family Yahtzee championship?" Brenna tilting her face to look up at him. "How did I not know this?"

"He doesn't win very often," Emily supplied. "So he probably doesn't want to advertise it."

Brenna laughed at Colt's frown. "Well, maybe today is your lucky day."

At that, his frown turned to a smile. "Every day's a lucky day when I'm with you."

Emily rolled her eyes. Brenna straightened and put her hand over her heart. "Sweet talk will get you all kinds of points. Except in the championship game," she said with a smirk.

They all laughed and nearly missed the knock on the front door. "Are you expecting someone?" Colt asked his mother.

"No." She got up from her seat and Colt stood with her. Brenna followed them to the hallway, but hung back a little. It would look odd if three people answered.

Nora opened the door and a man stood on the porch, his hands clasped behind him. "Yes?"

"I'm so sorry to bother you on Christmas Day." Sam's voice filtered through to the hallway where Brenna was standing. "But I've been tasked with bringing Captain Mitchell and Ms. Wilson with me. It's a matter of national security."

Colt stepped around his mother and held the doorknob. "What's this about Sam?"

"I've got a helo waiting on the outskirts of town. It's time-sensitive." Sam grimaced. "I'm really sorry, but I was told to have you bring all of your belongings."

Brenna's stomach sank. That meant they probably weren't coming back. Their holidays were being cut short. Probably because something had happened with Jassim. Or the emir. Or maybe even Nazer. She turned away from the door and went to the guest room to get her things, disappointment rolling through her. She'd been looking forward to getting to know Colt's family and having some downtime. Maybe even seeing her dad. But this was the profession she loved. She was good at it. If she could help take down a terrorist, she'd do it, no matter what it took.

When she was done throwing her things back into her bag, she rolled her small suitcase down the hall. Colt was getting his coat on. When his eyes met hers, she could see the apology in them. She shook her head. It wasn't anyone's fault. They'd chosen this life.

"We've got to go." Colt walked forward and took her suitcase handle from her. "The helo is on standby."

"I heard." She stopped in front of Colt's mom. "Thanks for breakfast. I'm sorry about all this."

Nora reached out and hugged her. "I understand. It's part of the job. But I'm so happy I had both of you for even a short amount of time. It made my Christmas perfect." She drew Colt into the hug, then Jack and Emily joined them as well. After a family group hug, with lots of 'I love you' to go around, and more promises to call as soon as they could, Colt and Brenna walked to Sam's car.

A police escort was behind him and Brenna's eyes widened. "What do you think this is all about?"

"I have no idea." Colt opened the back door and she got in. He slid in next to her. Sam waited until the police cruiser moved in front of them, lights flashing. Then both cars sped away. "Sam, can you tell us what's going on?" Colt asked.

"Sorry. I'm just supposed to bring you in as fast as possible." He maneuvered the car around a sharp turn.

"Is it about Jassim?" Brenna prepared herself for the answer. If Jassim had died, that could have international ripples.

"No, the doctors think he'll be fine. It was touch and go for a while there, though." Sam pulled up next to a field where a helo was idling. "You better hurry."

Colt and Brenna got out of the car. Sam popped the trunk so they could grab their suitcases. Running for the bird, they climbed on board and were airborne in minutes. The trip was short, and soon they were above Dwyer Hill Base.

"I haven't been to Dwyer since I finished training." Colt watched as they landed. JTF2 operators were based here, so this would be a homecoming of sorts for him.

Two officers were waiting to escort them onto the base and Colt and Brenna were whisked to an ops center. Colonel Hayes met them at the door, then ushered them to a large screen on the side of the room, where Julian's face stared back at them.

"Sorry to interrupt your Christmas plans," Julian said. His voice was steady, but his eyes were grim. "We found the address of Nazer's meeting in Idlib, but it's a fortress. There's no way we can breach this without a small army."

Every muscle in Brenna's body tensed in frustration. It was a never-ending cycle. No matter what they did, Nazer always managed to stay out of their reach.

Julian folded his hands on the small table in front of

him. "We have an asset who can get inside and at least give us eyes and ears for the meeting, but he needs some sort of password to get in." He leaned forward, his eyes zeroing in on Brenna. "We've only got a small window to get the asset in place, so I need you to think back to what Jassim said while you were with him. Did anything sound like a password?"

All eyes turned to Brenna. She resisted biting her lip or her fingernails, and focused on diving back into her memory. What had Jassim said? "The only thing that seemed out of the ordinary was when he was calling for his mother and then he said change is coming. He repeated that several times and didn't want her to leave his side."

"Change is coming. That could be it." Julian drummed his fingers on the table in front of him. "Can you think of anything else? We'll only have one shot at this and if the asset gives the wrong password, he'll be shot."

Brenna shook her head. "Beyond that, Jassim was just worried about stopping the meeting."

They listened while Julian relayed the information to someone else in the room who wasn't in camera range. "We're going to go with 'change is coming,' then." The lines around his eyes tightened, testifying to his worry. "Now we wait."

Julian tapped a few keys on the laptop. The screen changed to the hidden camera the asset was wearing, and the images it was picking up as he approached the meeting place. The building Nazer had chosen was a stone two-story with small doors and windows. The dozens of guards running security in the hallway and surrounding the building were more than Brenna had ever seen for a meeting like this. Nazer and his terrorist friends were being extra careful on this one.

The asset moved through the first two layers of guards and was now climbing the stairs to the room where the meeting would take place. He was breathing hard, but Brenna couldn't tell if it was from fear or exertion. He approached the guard outside the meeting room door and was asked for the password. Everyone held their breath.

This was it.

The asset repeated, "Change is coming." The guard was still for a moment too long and Brenna wanted to turn away. She'd been wrong. That wasn't the password. The asset would be killed right in front of them. She didn't want to watch.

But instead, the guard moved aside and opened the door for him. Both her and Colt breathed a simultaneous sigh of relief, their eyes now riveted to the screen.

When the asset walked in, his hidden camera revealed Tariq Hammam, Abu al-Masri, and Nazer sitting on large pillows at a low table. Four other men stood behind them. All talk ceased as they looked up at the asset's entrance. Nazer frowned. Standing, he walked over and stood in front of the asset, his face framed on the screen.

"Who are you?" he asked, his eyes narrowing. "What is your business here?"

Brenna couldn't help the ripple of fear for the asset. Did he have a cover?

"I'm here as a representative of Jassim al-Marisi. He's asked me to make sure the weapons are delivered to you and that all the agreements are honored." The asset bowed to Nazer, which seemed to appease him somewhat.

"Is the little whelp questioning my honor?" Nazer sneered, his face back onscreen. "Everything will be as agreed upon." He stared into the hidden camera for a heartbeat too long and Brenna saw the flash of recognition in his eyes. He knew. Somehow he knew the asset was wired.

"Get your guy out of there," Brenna said, urgency in her tone. "His cover's been blown."

But Nazer had already pulled out a smoke grenade and threw it at their asset. He dove behind the table just as the room erupted into chaos. The grenade exploded and smoke poured out. Their inside guy started coughing, and was barely able to keep Nazer in his sights from his position on the floor. He quickly stood.

"There's an opening in the wall," he choked out. The coughs were getting worse, but the asset was able to turn and give them a view of the room. His camera showed Nazer's smoky shadow sliding through a hidden door in the corner. The rest of the men in the room were coughing and falling over themselves trying to leave. One attempted to go the same way Nazer had, and the rest ran for the door.

Go after Nazer, Brenna wanted to yell. *He's the primary target. Don't lose him.*

Julian's voice came over the comms, saying out loud what Brenna had been thinking. "Follow Nazer, but be careful."

The asset climbed into the tunnel that Nazer had used. Inching carefully along the dimly lit passage, he came to the first turn and stopped. Looking down, a cell phone came into view on camera. Could Nazer have dropped it? Pocketing the phone, the asset moved forward, but soon came to the end of the tunnel. It led to the street. The now *empty* street.

Nazer had disappeared again.

With an inward sigh, Brenna tamped down her disappointment. They'd missed their chance to listen in on the meeting. Nazer had gotten away. Would they ever be able to capture him?

Julian instructed the asset to bring the phone in and to be careful getting back to the command center. Then he was facing Colt, Brenna, and Hayes onscreen.

"At least we got something. Hopefully that phone will tell us where Nazer is headed." Julian sucked in a breath. He cocked his head to the side, regret in his tone. "I know I said you could spend the holidays in

Canada, but I need both of you back here ASAP to help us dissect this new intel. And comb our contacts in Syria, in case Nazer decides to stay for a while. The jet is fueled and ready for you."

Colt glanced at her and gave a half-shrug. Duty called. "We're on our way. See you soon."

She bent her head, knowing that was the right call, but part of her wished she could have seen her father. The other part reminded her that he might not remember who she was and her heart ached at the thought. Maybe heading back to work was best after all.

Colonel Hayes moved closer and shook hands with both her and Colt. "Let's get that drink next time you're in town."

"Yes, sir." Colt faced his old commanding officer. "And sir, thank you for training me so hard. It saved my life more than once."

"Glad to hear it." The colonel's voice was gruff, but Brenna could tell he was warmed by Colt's words. A commanding officer who demanded the best from his men probably didn't hear thanks very often. "Be safe out there," he added as Colt and Brenna turned to leave.

"Always," Colt said with a smile as they walked out the door, back the way they'd come. He took her hand as they made their way to the exit. "I'm sorry, Bren," he said softly.

"We're together. That's all that matters." She leaned

into his side. "But I think you dodged a bullet on the Yahtzee tournament. I was planning on impressing you and your family with my Yahtzee skills."

"You've impressed me from the day we met." His grin faded and he stopped to face her. "Your father's care center is on the way to the airfield. Do you want to stop in?"

Brenna's chest felt tight. She wanted to say yes. But all the 'what ifs' crowded into her head. *Stop it*, she scolded herself. She'd faced down one of the most wanted terrorists in the world, interrogated hardened men who'd wanted to kill her and everyone who loved freedom. Compared to that, visiting her father shouldn't be so hard. She could do this.

Squaring her shoulders, she lifted her chin and looked up at Colt. "Okay. Let's go."

CHAPTER NINE

Colt sat in the back of the car with Brenna. It hadn't taken too much convincing to have Sam drive them to the care center to see her dad before they took off, but Brenna hadn't spoken since they'd gotten on the road. Her lips were pursed, her hands were clenched tight in her lap, and her knee was bouncing. She was a ball of anxiety and tension from her head to her feet. He wished he could ease that for her, then remembered something that might help.

He reached into his pants pocket to get out the gift he'd gotten for Brenna. "I got you a little something," he said, handing it to her with a smile. "Though I imagined giving it to you under a Christmas tree and not in a military vehicle."

"Knowing us, we probably should have expected that." She took the small jewelry box, her eyebrows raised. He could see the question in her eyes. This wasn't an engagement ring, though he hoped to buy her one of those sooner rather than later. He wanted to ask her father for his blessing first, but with his Alzheimer's diagnosis, that might not be possible. Today, he was going to focus on the good, though.

Brenna removed the ribbon and opened the lid. Drawing out the bracelet, she held it up and let out a little gasp. "Oh, Colt, it's beautiful."

Brenna touched each one of the little charms. An Eiffel Tower for Paris, the CN Tower for Canada, the British House of Parliament for England, and a minaret for Afghanistan. Every significant place they'd been together in the last few months.

"A charm for each of our adventures so far. And I hope to add a lot more." He took the bracelet from her and helped her put it on.

"Thank you." She looked at her wrist, then him. "It's perfect." She reached into her coat pocket and pulled out a small box. "I got you something, too."

He took the gift from her and opened the top. Inside was a watch, one that had a compass. "It's engraved on the back," Brenna said with a half-smile.

Colt turned the watch over. "*So you can always find your true north.*" He leaned forward and kissed her. "Maybe you're my true north," he murmured. Color heightened in her cheeks, but she didn't say anything, just smiled and watched him put it on. "I love it. Thank you," he said.

Leaning back, Colt put his arm around her and gently rubbed her shoulder. "Ready to see your dad?"

"I'm scared," she admitted. "What if he doesn't know me?"

"You'll know him. And I'll be right there with you." Colt tucked her closer against him. Seeing her father was going to be hard for her. Alzheimer's was devastating, but he wanted to help Brenna face whatever was coming.

"I'm ready." She nodded as if to emphasize her words.

Sam pulled up in front of the care center and Colt and Brenna got out. It was a well-kept one-story building with a few benches set strategically outside. The walks were clear of snow and there was a sculpture of a family near the front entrance. Colt took Brenna's hand and they stepped inside. The large lobby had a decorated Christmas tree with several couches and chairs placed nearby. There was also a fireplace boasting a large garland that smelled of pine. They walked to the nurses' station where a woman sat behind a desk. Once they'd signed in, the woman looked at her name on the clipboard.

"Your father is in the atrium," the nurse told Brenna. "It's his favorite room here."

Brenna nodded, and they turned down the hall the nurse had pointed to. She was gripping his hand so tightly, his fingers were white. He leaned in close. "It's going to be okay," he whispered. Her eyes met his, and she took a few deep breaths.

Colt opened the door to the atrium and ushered her through, his hand at the small of her back. Her father sat in the middle of the room, soaking up a bit of sunshine shining down from the skylight, his head tilted upward as if to catch every last ray. Brenna watched him for a moment before she started over to him.

"Dad?" Her voice was tentative, as if she wasn't sure what to expect.

He turned his face to her and recognition flooded his features. Standing, he held out his arms. Brenna didn't hesitate and stepped into her father's embrace. Tears rolled down the older man's cheeks.

"I'm so glad you're okay. I've missed you," he whispered, kissing her hair.

Colt watched them together. Her dad looked the same, just older and more frail. But he still had his military bearing. When they'd broken apart, Brenna turned to him, brushing away her tears.

Colt gave her a reassuring smile and held out his hand to her dad. "Good to see you, sir."

The two men shook hands. "I don't think I caught your name." Her dad furrowed his brow. "Have we met?"

"I'm Colt Mitchell, sir. I'm here with Brenna." He met her dad's gaze---he was staring hard at Colt.

Then his face suddenly brightened. "I've met you

before. Five years ago, when Brenna brought you home." He looked over at her. "Was it five years? Have you been dating all that time?" His brows knit together again and his foot started to tap.

"No, Daddy. We lost contact and just recently found each other again." She gave Colt a watery smile. "We're home for Christmas."

Her father gave a great sigh, a faraway look stealing over his face. "I miss the days when you would come running down the stairs, your braids flying out behind you, yelling 'It's Christmas!' Your mom would smile and laugh, and we'd watch you open your gifts. Remember that?"

Brenna nodded. "Mom always loved decorating the tree. Stringing popcorn, listening to Christmas music, and singing along---out of tune." She sniffed. "I miss her."

"Me, too, my girl." He took her hand and squeezed.

Brenna looked back at Colt, obviously thrilled that her dad had recognized her and was clear on what was happening around him today. Her happiness was the best Christmas present he could have gotten.

She gently pulled her dad back to the bench he'd been sitting on and handed him a small double frame, hinged in the middle. "Merry Christmas, Dad."

He stared down at the frame for a moment. On one side was a picture of their ranch house, and the other was a picture of the three of them, her mom, dad, and her. Tears filled his eyes as he looked at them. "I wish I could go back in time," he whispered.

"Oh, Daddy." Brenna laid her head on his shoulder. "I love you."

"I love you, too." He blinked rapidly and slipped his arm around her, hugging her to him. "Never forget that. No matter what happens." He looked up at Colt, his eyes piercing. "I think I asked you once before, but I want to ask you again. What are your intentions toward my daughter, young man?"

Colt swallowed. This wasn't exactly how he'd imagined asking for his blessing, but since her father seemed lucid, and Colt didn't know when they'd get back to Canada, he had to take the opportunity. "With your permission, sir, I'd like to be part of your family someday, with Brenna as my wife." He looked at Brenna when he said the words. Should he kneel? Take her hand? But his feet seemed rooted to the floor. "I love you, Bren. With my whole heart."

She stood and threw her arms around him, pressing her face into his neck. "I love you, too. I never stopped."

Her dad cleared his throat. She turned and gave him a nod. He slowly got to his feet. "I'll give my blessing on one condition: that you promise to love and take care of her always."

"I promise." Colt kept her close to him, wanting to savor this moment with her at his side.

Brenna's arm tightened around his waist. "Colt

always keeps his promises, just like you, Dad," she assured him.

Colt couldn't hold in his happiness, his heart overflowing with the feelings he had for Brenna. He bent to kiss her forehead. "Merry Christmas, sweetheart."

She went up on tiptoe and lightly kissed his lips. "It *is* a merry Christmas. Just like you said it would be," she murmured.

Holding her gaze for one more moment, Colt finally turned to face her dad. "Now that we're all family, I have to ask: Do you play Yahtzee? I'm trying to find someone to practice on so I'm not the weak link anymore."

Her father's eyes twinkled. "I sure do. And I'm happy to help you with your strategy. Us military men have to stick together."

A squeak echoed through the room as the atrium door opened. They all watched Sam walk in. He didn't waste any time getting over to them, an air of urgency around him.

"I am so sorry," he said. "But things are heating up in . . . um . . ." he looked at Brenna's dad, obviously trying to choose his words carefully. "The theater of operations you were heading to. We have to go."

Brenna's smile dimmed a bit. "Already?"

Her dad took her hand in his. "It's okay, honey. I understand that you've got to go save the world. But it means everything to me that you came to visit." His voice was low and filled with emotion. "I love you."

Brenna put her arms around him and hugged him. When she pulled back, she touched her dad's cheek. "I love you, too, Daddy."

Colt reached out to shake her dad's hand, but got pulled into a hug instead. "Take care of my baby girl," her dad said gruffly.

"I will." Colt patted the older man's back and they said their goodbyes. Sam was holding the atrium door, giving them some space to say goodbye, but also subtly reminding them they needed to hurry.

Colt intertwined his fingers with Brenna's as they walked past the Christmas tree in the lobby. The lights and ornaments seemed to shine a little brighter than when they'd first arrived.

"I'm going to sleep the entire flight to Syria," Brenna said with a yawn, pressing against his arm.

He chuckled, remembering how she'd wanted him to sleep on the way here. "You've definitely earned it."

He opened the door and kept her close as they headed toward Sam's car. This wasn't the Christmas he'd been expecting, but it was one he'd never forget. Even in the short time they'd had, he'd remembered how important the love of his family was and how lucky he felt to have Brenna at his side. He'd never take any of that for granted again.

That was his Christmas promise to himself.

OTHER BOOKS IN THE GRIFFIN FORCE SERIES

ABOUT THE AUTHOR

Julie Coulter Bellon is the author of over two dozen romantic suspense books. Her novel All Fall Down won the RONE award for Best Suspense, Pocket Full of Posies won a RONE Honorable Mention for Best Suspense and The Captain was a RONE award finalist for Best Suspense. Most recently, her books The Capture and Second Look were both Whitney finalists for Best Suspense/Mystery.

Julie loves to travel and her favorite cities she's visited so far are probably Athens, Paris, Ottawa, and London. In her free time she loves to read, write, teach, watch Hawaii Five-O reruns, and eat Canadian chocolate. Not necessarily in that order.